PASSION

Part One of the Willow Series

Abbey K Davies

Printed in the United States.
Published by: Abbey K Davies
Copyright 2012 Abbey K. Davies
All rights reserved.
ISBN-10:0977035026
ISBN-13:987-0-9770350-2-1

Dedication

I dedicate this book to those who have been abused by someone they love. Never allow anyone to take away who you are.

To all of the people who have loved and lost. Despite the hurt and pain, you will find your way again as long as you never give up.

To all the people who believe in love; True Love, Healthy Love, it is out there and you deserve it.

To all who have given me love, and to those who have hurt me, I forgive you.

To my beautiful children, Austin and Emily, may you always be surrounded by love.

Acknowledgements

This book has been inside of me for 20 years. I thank my dad for giving me the confidence to write a fiction book. I thank my mom for always supporting my passion and me.

My husband, for being alone while I was locked up writing and giving me the courage to write something that was once out of my comfort zone.

To my children for giving me all the space and time I needed, I love you.

To my Chiropractor and massage therapist for helping me with pinched nerves and carpal tunnel from writing.

A very special thanks to my best friend for reading as I wrote and for being there for me no matter what. For my editor for taking all the time she did to help make this book what it is. Thank you to you all, I love you!

Abbey

Introduction

Brooke Walsh is from a small New England town. She's the youngest of four kids, two sisters and a brother. She didn't mind being the youngest as it made her feel protected. Brooke was a person that always saw the good in people and was more than willing to lend a hand. As early as 5th grade, she began volunteering to help with the special needs children, known in her school as "the little kids." She also became a walking buddy to a little boy with Down syndrome, a friendship that lasted years.

She was extremely social in school, loved to have a good time and was often the life of the party. She had her clique, but she was also friends with people outside of her group. She didn't shy away from anyone. Everyone knew Brooke as the charismatic do-gooder girl. Being the way she was, didn't always benefit her; she often was shit on, from guys and girls alike. As popular as she was, it was ironic how little self-esteem she truly had.

Brooke not only has a huge personality, she is beautiful as well, but that was something she never saw in herself. She's petit, with brown hair that always seemed to shine, light brown cat eyes, and eyelashes that were resemblance of a camel. Many found her mysterious because of her vulnerable shyness that lay hidden deep within her. She used her sense of humor to make friends, going above and beyond to make others happy.

Brooke's senior year in high school was the year of change for her; for at eighteen, she was the only one of her friends that held ownership of her virginity. It was always a topic of conversation who was going to take her innocence. There were even bets by her guy friends as to when and with whom she would lose her innocence. First learning about it, she was pissed, but eventually she liked all the attention; it made her feel wanted. While the boys were betting, the girls were hating on her. Despite her charisma and endearing qualities, she still lacked confidence. Even her girlfriends often took advantage of this; knowing she would do anything to help another person.

It was no secret that Brooke had it hard for Josh since the end of her junior year. He was a friend, but she fantasized more than once about him. He was an amazing baseball player and she often found herself drooling at the sight of him in his perfect tight white uniform; showing all that he possessed. He had golden brown hair and deep blue eyes. He was on the shorter side, about 5 feet four inches and his body was rock solid.

Josh was so cute and he had this smile which showed his true personality… devious. Many girls in the school liked Josh with his devious, dynamic personality, which only fed his cockiness. Her girlfriends told her repeatedly to stay away from him, but the challenge and the draw was too much. She saw goodness hidden beneath his cocky, rock solid exterior and wanted others to see it too. She couldn't stay away.

Josh knew of her virgin status and wanted to be the one to take ownership; there were bets on the table after all. Brooke ignored her friends and pursued him anyway. Naïve about sex and intimacy, she never thought anyone would just take her innocence to win a bet. Not only did that year change her, but it also made her feel worse about herself. After graduation, she went off to college where she was excited to start anew, still with a heavy heart over Josh. That love affair was over, she was in a new place with all new people except for Noelle and she had to get over Josh. She was determined to focus on her academics and not get caught up with a guy.

She would never have gone looking on her own after her broken heart, but Noelle had a plan. Brooke never could have foreseen what was going to hit her when she met Jonathon. He was of pure beauty, possessing soft brown hair, cut perfectly over his ears, with eyes like hot chocolate. His lips were full and supple. His body was slender but muscular in all the right places and his ass could burn a hole in your eyes.

Jonathon was the president of his fraternity and the vision in nearly all the girl's dreams. He was a work of art in more than one way, but he had secrets; ones that should have been divulged before they were introduced by Noelle. Noelle had more plans than just a set up. She no longer could sit by and witness Brooke's goodness.

Josh knew I liked him. He flirted with me at times and finally one night we ended up kissing. I got his attention. One night led to many nights ending up together, not going past first base and he was okay with that it seemed. He finally made it to second base with me and I felt as if rocket ships were going overhead. I wanted more from him. He was a challenge, although we were often together, he seldom spoke to me at school or in front of people; he had an image to protect.

One September night a friend of mine was having a house party. This was the night. He wasn't going to wait forever. I walked up to the two-story house and entered. All eyes glared at me with dropped mouths. Tonight I wasn't the typical Brooke; wearing a white silky shirt, black skirt and a fire red thong with a garter belt. I was feeling hotter than hell and ready to show Josh I was ready. I grabbed my friend and we headed straight for the keg in the kitchen and the table full of shots being poured from the iced luge. With each shot I kept reminding myself that I was sexy and ready. Eventually we started playing quarters. I was pretty good at it. As we played, my confidence began to soar. My mind and body were heating up and my inhibitions were dwindling.

"Hey sexy, you look incredible tonight. Do you know what I want to do," Josh says while coming up behind, wrapping his arms around me and whispering and breathing in my ear.

"Tell me Josh, what do you want to do?"

"I'd rather show you," he says in between kisses on my ear.

"What's keeping us," I asked with complete confidence and loss of inhibition.

Grabbing my hand quickly and yanking me, he pulled me out of the kitchen through the throngs of people loitering about and led me up the stairs to the bedroom. I was ready, I think. I knew Josh was completely the wrong guy for me, especially the one who was going to be my first. Oddly, none of that seemed to matter to me right now.

The beer and shots helped some but the insecurities swarmed my brain. He stopped outside the bedroom, grabbing the door handle and turned to me.

"Are you sure Brooke?"

Squeezing his hand, I nodded. I couldn't form any words. As he turned to push the door open, I took a long deep breath, briefly closing my eyes. [You can do this Brooke you love him.] We stepped into the room and shut the door. It was clearly the spare bedroom of the house. The walls painted a neutral tan. There was a picture of a meadow over the bed but everything else was bare. The ceiling fan over the bed was humming and the window shades were down. The room smelled of strawberry potpourri, refreshing and clean.

"Brooke, it'll be okay.I promise I won't hurt you."

I smiled and he took my hand and brought it to his lips. Still in the upright position in front of the queen sized bed with a cream-colored bedspread.

"Josh, I'm a little nervous."

"Don't be. It's me and you know you want this and so do I."

He started kissing my neck and blowing in my ear and whispering sweet things and he laid me on the bed. His hard body got on top of mine. Continuously checking to see if I was okay and promising he wouldn't hurt me.

It started with kissing and hands softly roaming up and down my body. Our tongues started a sweet waltz but quickly became a rumba of desire and need. As our kisses became deeper and harder, my hands could no longer stay intertwined in his hair; they began to make their way across his hard, muscular back. My lower half begged for more. Josh must have sensed my urge. He reached under the hem of my skirt and unclasped the clip of my garter belt and released it so he could feel my warmth between my thighs. I was wet and physically ready but my brain hadn't caught up yet.

I pulled him closer to me and began stroking him and he moaned along with me. He was kind and gentle with me, "It'll be okay Brooke, I'll be gentle." In this moment, he made me feel special and not just a bet or a conquest. My brain caught up and I begged him for more. He entered me slowly. I moaned and tears fell down my face. I felt pain but I wanted to continue. This is who I have chosen to be my first and I didn't want to be made fun of if I chickened out. My virgin tightness around him and the newness to him made him erupt quickly.

I lay there with blood underneath me. I felt completely alone. It was a feeling I never felt before. Everything has now changed for me. I'm no longer a virgin and I'm changed. My body felt as if it was no longer mine. I got up out of the bed, put my clothes back on, put my garter and hose in my purse and went home and cried. He was kind to me but I felt somewhat empty, embarrassed and ashamed.

With Brian Adam's Song, 'Cuts like a Knife' playing in the background while I was taking a shower, I felt a connection to the song. I turned up the heat as much as possible because suddenly I felt dirty. I lathered soap repeatedly over my body and for a split second I thought I could wash it all away. I couldn't wash it away. I'm forever changed and this is a new realm for me.

About an hour after I was home, the phone rang, and it was Josh. "Hello?" "Hey," his voice sounds husky and uncertain; "Are you okay?" there was a pause, "Are you hurting?" Fire crept up to my cheeks and I was thankful he couldn't see me. "I hope you aren't hurting, I didn't mean to hurt you if you are."

With fear in his voice of the idea that he had hurt me physically, he apologized. He now feels guilty that he took such a precious ownership from me. Reassuringly, he said to me, "The next time will be much better and it will only get better after that."

I breathed a sigh of relief thinking he must want more from me if he is talking about our next time. Maybe he feels the way I do, I can only hope.

"Josh, I just feel changed you know and I need to

be alone."

"I understand Brooke; please tell me you're okay."

"Yes, Josh I'm okay, it's hard to explain."

Back at school on Monday, I was nervously walking the halls with paranoia that everyone who passed by me knew I was no longer a virgin, that I got laid. I hadn't told any of my girlfriend's yet and I was praying that Josh hadn't told his buddies either but that was a wish only and not fact, which was soon to be proven.

In the cafeteria, the guys were giving high fives to each other and saying, "The bets are off, Josh won," it bombarded me. I sank down in the bench and put my head down in complete horror. It was just a bet and nothing more. I felt completely used and worthless. Josh suddenly walked in, saw the crowd whispering and glanced at me with his smile that ran through my veins like fire. I couldn't even speak to him.

At the end of the school day, walking out to the parking lot, I noticed Josh leaning up against my car. I wanted to run the other way. I was humiliated and my gut was about to explode but instead I took small steps toward the car. All the while with butterflies in my belly and beads of sweat starting to form on my brow. When I got up to the car and unlocked the door, he got in the passenger's side and told me to drive. My hands were trembling and lips couldn't open to say a word.

He directed me where to go. I drove down winding back roads in this beautiful New England town; I had never been on these roads before. "Stop when we get to the empty field," his voice commanding. There was nothing but open space surrounded by trees, it reminded me of a corral but with trees. The field was private. It was sanctuary like. Beautiful and peaceful but why was he taking me here?

Stopping the car, I put my head down; I was embarrassed to look at him. He grabbed my chin and turned my face to look him in the eye. The flow of tears were trickling down my face. He wiped my tears and began to kiss me. I tried to pull away but I had no strength to fight it. I was in love with him. He moved from my lips to my ear and whispered, "You were not just a bet, you were beautiful and you gave me a gift." He moved his lips from my ear back to my mouth where I could barely breathe any more.

Finally, he took my hand, kissed it, and said, "Follow me." He reached in the back seat, knowing I always had a blanket in the back and grabbed it. Walking carefully through the trees into the open field, I had no idea what he had planned. I just knew I was in trouble. I knew I couldn't resist him. Even when my mind knew he was all wrong for me. My heart and mind were not in sync.

He set the blanket out and pulled me down to him. There were no words, just stares. I wanted to talk about it and he had other ideas. He was now the only one I was familiar with and he knew it and wanted more. He was not a talker or not one that talked about feelings and emotions. This was an obstacle for me as I loved to talk things over, all too much at times.

We lay on the blanket and the sun was peeking over the trees on this beautiful September day. I was frozen with fear, desire, confusion and disgust in myself. He ran his fingers through my hair and moved down to behind my ear, which he knew was a weak spot for me. He continued to caress my weak spot and then kissed me gently on the ear, then to the neck. I tried to speak and stop him but he took my mouth to his to disable my voice and I began to tremble.

I could feel my small breasts perking up and nipples getting hard with desire. He took notice and tickled his fingers around them, enjoying watching me squirm. I ran my hands through his thick brown hair and then kissed his ears and his chest, which was of perfect muscle. He then followed the trail down my body with his hands and then his tongue. I became scared and tried to push him away from going any further. This was all so new to me.

He grabbed my hands and held them behind my head so I could no longer fight it, but he knew I really wanted him. With his other hand he unbuttoned my jeans and moved his hand down my pants to my opening. He put one finger in and he could tell I was enjoying it so he continued. He then pulled my pants and panties all the way off and pulled his pants down. My hands still locked behind my head and I had no control. He put a condom on with one hand and put his hardness in me. There were no words, just eye contact and pleasurable sounds that made me even more nervous.

He whispered in my ear, "This is how it was supposed to be." I then clutched him as he released my arms and he came. After, he turned me over, rubbed my back and my butt cheeks and thighs. There were still no words, just touch. We lay there together for about an hour looking at the blue sky, without a word spoken. "What the fuck," I was saying to myself.

After an hour, he pulled me to my feet, walked me back to the car and roughly said, "Drive me home." He turned the music off and it was an awkward silence. I couldn't drive fast enough. The tension was so thick and my mind was wandering and I needed to burst into tears but I couldn't have him see me. I didn't know if I wanted to cry because it was beautiful or because there was pure silence. I was feeling all alone, once again. I drove into his driveway; he looked in my eyes, and spoke, "Next time, will be even better."

Driving home, my mind was swirling but my body felt satisfied. Confusion was thick as fog. I wasn't in control and had no idea what this relationship was. I did know that I really wanted to be with him. I wanted to be his girlfriend. I'm not sure if it's so strong because he is a challenge or was I in love with him?

Josh's and my sexual encounters went on for a long time. I did love him. As much as you can truly know about love at this age but I was never sure how he felt about me other than the sex. I just knew that he was the only one I had been with intimately. Even though he was a bad boy and was never that kind to me, I always went to him. I was loyal to him but he didn't reciprocate. I was more of a convenience fuck for him. He was good to me when we were alone but in company I was non-existent. Having the same group of friends was an advantage and a disadvantage for me. We saw each other often but never a planned date or anything. At the end of the nights we always found our way to each other.

Noelle Green and I were friends in High School and are now college roommates. Noelle and I don't share the same morals or opinions on many things. Noelle was promiscuous and had many lovers. She couldn't count them all, nor name the names. I was often sad for her because she was stunningly beautiful but had no pride for her body and let guy after guy use her.

It was an interesting combination of roommates. Noelle was from a wealthy family and me, middle class. Noelle's closet was full of designer clothing, which was a benefit to me as we wore the same size. I never felt as pretty as her but I knew that I was respectable and that mattered to me more than looks.

Within the first few weeks of college, Noelle had already found her prey. At a fraternity party she went missing and left me alone in the dark basement that smelled of wet socks and beer. I didn't have to think much about what she was doing, I just didn't know with whom.

I walked up to the third floor looking for her and I saw a line of guys outside of a room. I asked, "What are you guys in line for?" One guy turned and said, "Pussy." I, completely red in the face and not grasping that there was a girl behind the door because I couldn't believe someone would do this. I continued on my search for Noelle but I was coming up empty. Walking back up to the third floor, I found myself asking, "Who is the girl behind the door?" One guy said, "Some hot blonde girl. I think her name is Noelle."

Noelle lay on the makeshift bed of this frat room and got fucked by one, two, and three…. eight guys. Each guy would walk out of the room with a smile, give a high five to the next in line and brag that they were one of the early birds.

I stayed down the hall crouched down in the corner, watching in horror what was transpiring. After number eight came out, Noelle followed. She saw me crouched down and said, "Let's go get a beer, I'm thirsty." I bet you are I was thinking to myself. As regular as any other minute. She never said a word about it and we went and got a beer.

We went back to our dorm room that night and I had no idea what to say and I decided to say nothing. This was my friend, albeit, different from myself but nonetheless my friend. Tossing and turning all night looking over to her in her bed and seeing her sleeping like a baby. I couldn't grasp what the night had been.

The next morning, we all went to class and then to a different fraternity party. Noelle and Pam from our dorm and I went to the party together. I told Pam, "Stay with me. Noelle will probably disappear." We danced under the disco ball and had too many beers from the warm keg. Noelle no doubt disappeared and this time I didn't go looking. She obviously had a mission and I couldn't be witness to it again.

Pam and I left the frat; went to a local convenience store, got some junk food and went back to our dorm room. We stayed up until 4 am and Noelle still didn't come back. In the morning I looked over to Noelle's bed and it hadn't been slept in. With the raging headache I had and the blurry vision, I wasn't sure if I was seeing things clearly. I got up out of bed and confirmed that she had stayed out the night. Her bed was still made from the previous day.

Later that afternoon Noelle resurfaced. She came in and gloated, "That was the best night of my life. I met the cutest guy and he's so sweet and he was a great fuck." I asked her if she was going to see him again or was this just another one-nighter and she embellished, "Oh yeah he was that good." She then told me he had a damn cute roommate and that I should meet him. I wasn't so sure about that. I was still a rookie at the sex thing and I felt unworthy of a real relationship after Josh.

Noelle continued to stay out all night and I stopped worrying. Pam and I stayed up studying together as we were both law majors. Noelle would come home to shower and get a change of clothes. I hadn't asked her if she was still with the same guy Nathan, but I hoped she was. She was happy and I guess that was what mattered.

Pam and I were up late studying for finals and a drunken Noelle came through the door, flopped herself on the bed and said, "I'm in love." Blah Blah. We were studying for our 8:30 Legal Research final. I asked Noelle if she was going to study and she said, "No, I don't need to. I have everything already." Finally, she passed out in her own bed that she hadn't slept in for months.

The alarm clock rang and it was a chorus of moans and groans from Noelle and me. I got up, put my hair up in a clip, put my sweats on, grabbed a pop tart and went out the door to my final. On my way to class I was thinking about the roommate Noelle had mentioned. She swore he was cute. I have to remind myself to ask her about him again when I get back.

Two hundred and forty questions on this final and my brain was fried. Thank god Pam and I made up songs to memorize everything. It was over and I went back to the dorm. On my bed there was a white piece of paper with my name on it. Noelle left me a note:

Hey Brooke,
There's an invite only party tonight at the
fraternity. I want you to meet Jonathon, Nate's

roommate. He is wicked hot!!! Meet me there. Oh and he has brown hair with really dark eyes, he's tall and built. He told me to tell you he would be wearing a black turtleneck. Meet me there at 8:00. Don't be shy and wear my leggings that are hanging in my closet and the long sweater with the orange, yellow and pink. Will be waiting for you downstairs...Noelle

Holy crap! I have to walk in there by myself and he knows I'm coming. I have butterflies and its hours away. She didn't call me and just left me with this note. I had to take a nap before this big party; my mind is going in a million directions. Excitement, fear, doubt and more fear encompassed my brain until I finally fell asleep.

Pam came in a few hours later and woke me up. I showed her the note from Noelle and she told me to go for it. She was all excited for me and said, "I'll do your hair. This Jonathon guy would be lucky to have someone as beautiful and sweet as you. Don't be nervous, just be who you are." She made me more at ease, so I took a shower and got ready for the makeover.

Scoffing down a bowl of oodles of noodles after blow drying my hair and waiting for the miraculous Pam to come and make me look beautiful. I put on the leggings and the sweater, looked in the mirror and was pleasantly surprised how the outfit looked on me. I pulled out a pair of black heels and put them on. Pam curled my hair. The whole time telling me to have sex. She said I needed it after final week. I yelled, "NO WAY! I've only been with one guy. I am not Noelle. It won't happen!"

The hairspray is sprayed, the perfume Beautiful, by

Estee Lauder is sprayed and I'm as ready as I will ever be. Before I hop in my car, all the girls in the dorm are wishing me luck and can't wait until I get home to tell them all about him. We all laughed and I drove away.

Driving over to the fraternity I had a nagging feeling in my stomach. I think I was excited and mortified at myself at the same time. I was intentionally going there to meet a guy. I sure hope that he's nicer than Josh was. I won't be someone's convenient screw anymore.

At the front door of the fraternity there was an invitation for me. They crossed my name off the list and I headed downstairs to meet Noelle. The only thing I am thinking is that I need a beer. I cannot believe I know what he's wearing and I'm sure he knows what I am since Noelle told me what to wear. I took a deep breath in, then a deep breath out.

How can this basement smell so bad when the party just started? It smells of men's cologne and strong perfumes mixed with stale beer. Everyone was trying to get lucky and I needed a beer. I walked over to the bar where the keg was and filled my cup, knocked it right back and refilled it. I needed the help. Along came Noelle and Nate. He's adorable as Noelle said and very nice. With my eyes moving all around, hoping not to see a guy in a black turtleneck, I tell Noelle, "This isn't a good idea." Noelle snickered, "You'll change your mind when you see him. Loosen up! My God, you and Josh are over and it's time to move on. Get over it already, I'm doing you a favor."

As I glance to my right, I see a guy in a black turtleneck. He's not too cute and he's acting like a dork. My blood is boiling at Noelle; I can't believe she wants to set me up with him. Calling her over, I said,

"I'm leaving; I'm not meeting that guy." Noelle laughed. "That's not him Brooke. I have better taste than that. Look into that room over there and you'll see him."

My eyes shift to the room off the dance room and I see this vision of perfection. It can't be him. He's perfect and he would never be interested in me. Back to the bar I go; meanwhile running directly into Nate. I told him, "I can't meet Jonathon; he is out of my league." "Brooke, yes you can; he's a great guy, funny, brilliant and he wants to meet you."

My eyes can't stop gazing into the other room and my heart is pounding along with my lower half throbbing. What is the matter with me? I haven't even met him yet. Finally, feeling a buzz and more relaxed, Nate and Noelle took me to the other room for the introductions. Holy Shit!

We said our hellos and the two of them left us. Nervous laughter takes over and my humor comes out in full force. Jonathon knew I was nervous and he rubbed my wrist softly and said, "It's okay, being fixed up is always awkward but I'm glad they had me meet you." My hand is trembling at the simple touch of his. I was smitten already. He was funny, he had gentle eyes and I was mesmerized by his movie star looks.

After a few hours at the party with Jonathon he asked me if I wanted to go to his room where it was quiet. Without a second thought I said yes and it was so out of character for me, but something was drawing me to him and I couldn't resist. We filled our beer cups before heading to the staircase and we saw Noelle and Nate passing by and smiling.

He opened the door to his room; it was dimly lit

with a lava lamp. There were two waterbeds under a loft, a small couch, stereo and two desks on top of the loft. It was small, intimate and comfortable. I sat on the couch and he handed me my beer, thankfully. He sat down beside me and put his soft supple lips on mine. It was gentle and perfect. I took my mouth away from his, I put my head down feeling anxious and completely out of my element. "Brooke, what's wrong?" "I'm nervous and I don't want you to think I am a slut." "I know the difference Brooke. I know you aren't a slut. I knew right away that you weren't like any other girl. I want you to relax and if you don't want to do something we'll stop. As hard as it may be for me, I will not make you do anything you don't want to," he said rubbing my hand.

He grabbed my hand and rubbed each finger one by one. It was simple and soothing. I then reached up to him and kissed him. He opened my mouth with his lips and our tongues met again. I could barely breathe but I wanted more. My legs were weakening and my lower half was getting hot and was burning for him.

He grabbed my hands, pulled me off the couch and ducked me under the loft onto his waterbed. I knew I couldn't hold back. There's some strong force pulling me to him. I had never felt this before. I just knew I needed more of him. He surely was not a rookie like me, no he was seasoned and he knew what he was doing. At the time it didn't even matter anymore because I was not stopping him.

Once on the waterbed it began sloshing and forming waves. He put himself on top of me and ran his fingers through my hair. Just looking down in my eyes, he grabbed my hair and put his lips on mine. His tongue was so smooth and moist. He moved his hand under my sweater and I flinched a bit. He began licking my nipples and then twisting them, adding a light bite. I gave out a moan of delight and he hoarsely said, "Does it feel good?" Panting, I mustered up a "Yes!"

I can feel his hardness through his jeans and I knew this was not as far as this was going tonight. I wanted him inside of me; I needed him inside of me. I was like a volcano waiting to erupt. He pulled my sweater over my head and was kissing and licking me all the way down to my happy trail. He told me not to move, to let him please me. I couldn't move if I wanted to. I was in a complete daze. He went over my folds briefly with his mouth and down to my inner thigh. He was rubbing and kissing and I couldn't be still. He gently pushed my bottom down so I was flat and began to rub my clit in a circular motion.

Breathing became labored and I had never felt this sensation before. I had no idea what was happening to me. He alternated between his tongue and his fingers on my clit and I was no longer in control of my body. He had full control. He put his finger in me and I couldn't imagine what was to happen next. My legs began to shake uncontrollably and I got an intense hot feeling in my stomach that I never felt before. My vagina became so hot and pulsating that I lost my breath. This was my first orgasm. With his seductive voice, "Brooke, you're okay. This is supposed to happen. Enjoy it and let yourself feel it. I want to make you feel good."

He brought himself back to me and kissed me and I could taste myself on his tongue. He put his hardness inside of me and fucked me hard and harder until he came and collapsed on top of me. All the years with

Josh, I guess I never had an orgasm and I just knew that I was going to need more. It was a sensation I could easily become addicted.

Still naked, he had his arm around me and my head was on his chest as we fell asleep. I had no idea what the morning was going to bring but no matter what, this was worth it. I feel like I lost my true virginity, only this time, with a guy that was flawless and there was an undeniable connection and it just felt right.

As he moved, the waterbed sloshed again and woke me up. I hid my face in the pillow like a shy toddler. He turned my head and kissed me softly on the nose. Shivers ran down my spine. His touch was a current going through my body right down to my toes. His touch affected every part of my body.

All I could smell was stale beer breath and sex. Our sex and it was awesome. Jonathon whispered to me, "Last night was amazing." I blushed, without saying a word.

Noelle and Nate woke up in the bed right next to us with a curtain as the only separation. Noelle opened the curtain and annoyingly squealed, "Hello kids, have fun last night?" Only she would have such little class. "It was a beautiful night," Jon said, licking his lips looking straight into my eyes.

Discussing what we all had to do that day, Noelle and I told the guys our mothers were coming to visit. They laughed and I was horrified that my mom was coming and I was lying in this bed with a stranger that I had had amazing sex with the night before. Noelle and I got up and got our things and left to get home and shower and ready for lunch with our moms. As I was walking down the hall of the fraternity I found myself wondering if I would ever hear from Jonathon again. Was this a one-night thing for him or would this turn into something more?

Noelle and I drove home together and she started the inquisition, "So how was your night? I told you he was hot. Did you fuck? You better have because he won't stick around if you didn't." What's that mean? I was thinking to myself. I told her we talked a lot and had a great night with no details as this was private.

The girls at the dorm were waiting anxiously by my door to see how my night went. Pam asked, "Did you meet him? Is he as hot as Noelle said," I answered, "Yes I met him and yes he was incredibly hot. He was perfect." Knowing that I didn't come home they assumed that there was sex but I wouldn't give any information.

We had to get ready for our visiting moms so the chitchat had to end with the curious girls. We both took showers, dressed and tidied up our room a bit so we wouldn't get a lecture from our moms. Our moms arrived and gave us hugs and kisses. When they came they always came with bags of treats for us. This time they came with treats and a microwave. We weren't allowed to have microwaves but we didn't care. We hid it behind all Noelle's clothes in the closet.

Off to lunch we went. My mom knows me like no other and I was tormented by the thought of her knowing I had mad passionate sex with some guy I met just last night. I hope Noelle won't say anything and my mother won't sense something about it.

The host sat the four of us in a booth. Happy it was

away from the crowd. Noelle blurted out that I had met a guy last night and I stayed the night. I was horrified. It didn't take her long; my mom turned to me and said, "Was he cute?" My body became like jelly just thinking about him and my answer was, "Beyond!"

We sat and talked and ate for a couple hours and Noelle was telling them about Nate. Of course it was always about her, but I was thrilled because the attention was off me. My mind began to relive the moments of last night, his kiss, his tongue, his fingers and hands over my body. This overwhelming feeling came over me; it was intense fear that I was yet another conquest.

I got up from the table and went into the bathroom to throw up. Between the thoughts of last night being a onetime encounter to the remnants of the beer, I was sick. I wanted to go home, curl up in my bed and make these thoughts stop.

Grateful that our moms came and brought goodies and we had a good meal, not dining hall food but I now just wanted to be alone. Never did I think that I'd ever have the alone feeling that I had after my first time with Josh and this was more intense. It couldn't be. I needed to learn everything about Jonathon and I wanted so much more with him than just great sex

Back at our dorm, we gave our mom's hugs and kisses and they went on their way. Noelle took my car over to Nate's frat and left me to be alone. Jealous in a way that she could just go over and be with him and knowing that Jonathon would be there, made me sicker in the gut. I changed my clothes and put on the sweater that I'd worn last night so I could smell him. I got into my bed and stared up at the ceiling when tears began to flow.

What was it about this guy that made me have to have him? I picture his eyes, the gentleness and fire that they had when he looked in to mine. I was yearning for him. My lip was quivering and I remember how my legs were shaking last night and that feeling I had in my stomach. It was A M A Z I N G! It was a feeling I never felt before. I wasn't in control of what was to happen next and it made me feel a bit uneasy and excited at the same time.

There was a knock on my door. The voice calling out I had a phone call. I assumed it was my mom saying it was great to see me. I went to the phone in the hall and I answered, "Hello." It wasn't my mom, it was Jonathon! Holy Shit, he's calling me. Jonathon, the guy in the black turtleneck is calling me.

"Hey, this is Jonathon. How was your day with your mom?" "Good, it was great to see her." "Do you have any plans for tonight," he asked. "No." "Good, do you want to get together?" "Sure, do you want to come to my dorm room?" "Sounds good, I'll see you at 7:00." Holy shit! He's coming over tonight.

Immediately, I ran and got Pam and told her. She was laughing at how nervous I was and came to help pick out my outfit. "Brooke, you wished he would call you and your wish has come true. Enjoy it. You're an amazing girl." "Pam, I know I wanted him to call. I'm just so damn nervous and I don't want to get hurt again. I want more than sex with him." "Brooke, don't live in fear, you never know what you could miss out on." "You're right Pam. I'll just be in the moment," I said thinking about what to wear.

I'm going for casual attire tonight. We'll be hanging out in my room. I grab my tight Calvin Klein jeans and a white button down shirt. This will be fine, comfortable and reserved. I ran to the store before he came, picked up some cheese and crackers and strawberries. When I got back, I sliced up the cheese, put the strawberries and cheese on a paper plate and had a roll of crackers alongside. Very fancy, college style hors d'ouvres.

Jonathon signed in with the dorm mother, who was 80 years old and came up the stairs to my room. Pam showed him to my room and of course, she was sizing him up. The knocking on the door made my stomach drop. I was sober, no beer goggles for him and I began to have a panic attack. I had to keep telling myself to take a deep breath, calm down its okay.

I opened the door and just stared at him. I can't speak and the sight of him cripples me. "Can I come in," he laughed. Completely embarrassed of my facial expression, I finally told him, "Sorry… come in." I was stumbling on my words and I didn't know what to say. What the fuck? He is so hot. He is even hotter than last night!

He knew I was a bit edgy, so he took both my hands into his and kissed them. He then wrapped his arms around me, "Brooke, last night was amazing." For some shocking reason, I looked into his dark eyes and said, "It was more than amazing, it was delicious."

We both laughed and sat down on the floor. The cheese and crackers and strawberries are set up on my pillow desk and we started to munch on that. He took a strawberry and brought it to my nose for me to smell, then down to my lips and he fed me. It was intense. I then did the same for him and he brought his lips to mine. Tasting of strawberry and lusciousness, I couldn't get enough. His hair was so soft and his eyes were melting my soul. On the floor we were kissing from slow to hard, tongue to no tongue. It was getting really hot in here.

After a while, we took a breather and started talking. Uncomfortable on the floor, we went and lay on top of my bed. The bed was rickety and loud. I feared someone would think something was going on. On the other hand, the old lady from downstairs would send one of her assistants up to check on the racket. Lord knows she couldn't climb those stairs luckily or he would've been thrown out. We shared childhood stories, laughed hysterically and made a connection that was undeniable. The whole time he was stroking my arm up and down and he was making me very hot. This guy put me in a hypnotic state. He was powerful and in control of me.

I reached my hand down his pants but he took it away and said, "Not tonight. This night is for us to get to know each other." Are you kidding me? I wanted more of last night. I wanted him inside of me, to feel his beautiful body on mine. Feeling a bit rejected, I pulled my hand back up to his and continued talking and laughing. Peace and comfort came over me and I realized this was not just about sex. It was so hard to refrain but he was again, in control. We laughed until tears fell through the night. The bed was creaking, not from sex but laughter.

Guys weren't allowed to stay in our all girl's dorm but we had Pam go sign him out and he stayed the night. We knew Noelle wasn't coming home so it was just the two of us. There was no sex, just gentle touches and passionate kisses in between our laughter. I know longer felt rejected, I felt treasured. This was better than sex; it was something I never felt before in my life. There were no bets, no conquests to be had and it was pure heaven with this beautiful guy.

We awoke in the morning with our clothes still on.
I brought him to the dining hall for breakfast and we
recapped some of the stories we had told last night and
laughed some more. He teased me and said, "You are
so damn cute." I felt like I was in a dream. When we
finished breakfast, we went outside by his car, he
kissed me long and hard and said, "Thank you." I
asked him, "Why are you thanking me?" "Brooke, I
have to be honest with you, in all my life I've never
had a night like that." My body was trembling. If I
could have, I would've taken him right in the middle
of the road. "I should be thanking you," I replied, and
we said our good-byes both smiling.

He had to get to class, so he said he would call me
later. I said okay. I was scared whether he would or
not. Walking back to my dorm, I was full of joy and I
was singing, Cindy Lauper's, "True Colors. I'm in
love! Full blown and how could this be happening so
quick? I couldn't come up with the answer but I knew
there was nobody else I wanted.

It was eleven thirty and I had class at noon. My
least favorite class. I thought about ditching but I
decided to go to eat up the time before Jonathon
called. Walking up the stairs into the building, there
was a group of three girls that were from the dorm
across the street from mine. They were talking about
some guy from the fraternity. When they saw me pass

them, I heard them say, "That's her." I turned around to the girls, and asked, "Are you talking about me?" Stuttering began and this girl Steph, a very tall, thick girl with bleached blonde hair gone badly, said, "Yes." "What are you talking about me for?" "I was just saying that you're the girl that is seeing Jonathon from the fraternity," she replied with a smug expression.

Having no idea how they would know that and why it was a topic of conversation. I didn't say much back and I went into class. Steph was in my class and I found her intimidating at the very least. She was so big compared to me and I just didn't have a good sense about her. She asked me how long this with Jonathon had been going on. I didn't think it was any of her business, so I didn't reply and the instructor finally came in.

All during class I was curious why they were discussing my relationship of any sort with Jonathon. Yes, he is hot, but was that all it was? Changing my thoughts to Jonathon, just wondering what he'd planned for tonight brought tingles in my lower region. I could only hope that tonight would involve more touch than last. After receiving my first ever orgasm, I was looking forward to more.

After class, I headed back to the dorm to find a note on my door that Jonathon called. So early I thought, he must be canceling. I called him back and the phone rang and rang until someone in the house answered. There were no phones in the rooms, just a main phone. After a few minutes, he came to the phone, "Hey, I just want you to be dressed properly tonight, being November, so dress warm." He wouldn't divulge anything about what we were doing but I agreed. "Oh and Brooke, can we take your car, mine won't start?"

"Sure no problem. I will pick you up then." "See you at seven, be ready to have fun," he said with a sexy slur.

I'm ready for sure. A tad less nervous now and full of excitement. He liked me, he really did. Noelle was in our room when I returned from the phone call and she was getting ready to go home with Nate for the weekend. I thought to myself how it was getting serious between them. I was happy for her and hopeful that she'd remain faithful. I told her I was going out with Jonathon tonight and he told me to dress warm. I asked her if she knew what he had planned and she just grinned.

Rummaging through my closet, I pulled out a pair of thick beige cords, a cream turtleneck and a black sweater, definitely not too sexy but indeed warm. I pulled my boots out from behind where we had the microwave hiding and put them on. I was ready for a cold night but hoping it would turn very hot.

His fraternity was only about a mile and a half away from my dorm, so the ride was short. I stopped at the convenient store and got some breath mints and some Kudos, they were my favorite. Taking a deep breath in while pulling into his parking lot. Suddenly feeling like a little kid on Christmas morning. I adjusted my coat and went inside to let him know I was there. He came down the stairs and I was in awe. He was wearing jeans, the same black turtleneck of that first night with a cardigan sweater over it. He was wearing an unzipped snow coat. He was simply incredible looking. When he got to the bottom step where I was standing, he looked briefly behind him, then kissed the tip of my nose and whispered, "Hello, I missed you."

He got in the driver's seat and I got in the passenger's side, shaking because just his presence made me feel so alive. "Where are we going," I ask nervously. With mystery in his voice, he just said, "Somewhere simple and quiet." Before pulling out of the parking lot, he remembered he had forgotten something, so he ran back in to grab it. He came back out to the car with a duffle bag. I was wondering what was in the bag. He noticed my curiosity and he told me I would see soon enough.

Darkness is setting in and he pulled into what looks like a private park. Is there even such a thing as a private park? He got out of the car, grabbed the duffle bag, and said, "Come on." I didn't hesitate. There was a huge Weeping Willow tree in the park and he led me underneath it, where in fact, it was private. The willow branches came down all around the trunk. How he knew about this, I wondered.

He laid down a blanket. This was the only blanket that he had on his bed, light blue, worn out comforter, but it was cozy. He told me to sit, so I did. He sat next to me and said, "I have something to tell you." For a brief moment, I thought back to the girls at school that were talking about him and me. Maybe he's going to shed some light on that. He took my hair, put it behind my ear and gave my ear a delicate kiss. Then he grabbed my face with both hands and kissed my lips, not opened lips, just soft pecks. I could tell he was prepping himself for whatever he wanted to say to me and I was getting increasingly anxious.

Jonathon began by saying, "There are a lot of things you don't know about me. I am not proud of everything I have done thus far in my life. However, when I saw you that first night come into the room, something happened to me. Your smile was infectious and you made me want to smile. Your innocence, at the same time as your powerful personality made me want this to be different. I knew when we went to my room and you were sitting on my couch that you were not what I was used to. At that moment, I knew I had to try my hardest to make you feel as I did."

I opened my mouth to speak and he put one finger on it to stop me, "I need to get this out. Brooke, I have such a comfort with you and to be blunt, I wasn't looking for anything more than a fuck at the mere mention of being set up. I have to tell you this isn't what I thought once I met you. Last night when we told each other our childhood stories and were laughing and just being together, I never had that with anyone. You made me feel like we had known each other forever and I want you to know, I want you to be all mine."

With a tear in my eye, I was now able to speak. "I was so scared to go and meet you and I was taken by your beauty when I saw you through the doorway. I wanted to run because I didn't think you would even look my way. Jonathon, I've only been with one other person intimately and what we did that first night was completely out of character for me. The night we were introduced, my whole body was screaming for you. My panties were wet from just saying hello," I laughed feeling embarrassed.

He laughed and I continued to say, "I feel something so magnetic toward you and I want to be yours and only yours." He reached below my butt and lifted me on to his lap. Immediately, I could feel he was growing hard underneath his jeans. He kissed my forehead, then my nose, and I loved that. I took his face in my hands and kissed one corner of his mouth, then to the next until he sucked my mouth into his. The passion was undeniable. His lips attached to mine; he managed to take my coat off as well as his. Seeing the black turtleneck again made me literally cream in my pants. What was it about that turtleneck? He moved down to my neck and sucked hard, leaving a mark and he said, "Now I know you're mine." I wanted nothing more than to be his and I was, from now on.

He went into the duffle bag and retrieved some lubricant that was supposed to get hot when applied. "I knew it would be cold out here and I wanted to warm you up," he said smiling sexily. "He thinks of everything," I said to myself. This guy could do anything to me. I wouldn't care and I hope he does.

It's completely dark outside and darker under the Weeping Willow Tree and I wanted to see his face. Out of his handy dandy duffle bag, he pulled out a lantern run by batteries. He placed it up by the top of the blanket and it shined a faint shine, but it was good enough to see and study his eyes and face. He lifted the lantern to my face and told me I was beautiful and he wanted more from me.

"What can I give you Jonathon; I will give you anything and all of me." He smiled and doted, "I don't want to leave anything left to the imagination with you. I want us to little by little, do everything together." With that said and the sparks that were igniting, he kissed me hard and brought my head to his lower half. It took but a second to figure out what he wanted from me. He wanted me to suck him, to give him a blowjob. Who was I to say no? I wanted him in every way possible.

He lay back, I am now between his legs and I start to stroke him softly and take him into my mouth. Up and down with my tongue, licking his balls and then back to his beautiful penis. While taking him deeper and deeper into my mouth, he's moaning with pleasure, as am I. Shocking me, he flips me over so I am sitting on his face. This was brand new for me and a bit uncomfortable as well.

He began to lick me as I'm swallowing the trickle of juices coming out of him. His tongue is very experienced and he is licking my clit and softly biting it and I can't hold back. At the same time, we both came in synchronicity. Fucking ecstasy!

This night wasn't over. We both wrapped up in the blanket and we held each other tight as if we were afraid we would be separated. Jonathon has now had me in the most intimate way I've ever been. I pleasured him as he pleasured me and it was inexpressible the chemistry between us.

After the exhaustion had worn off a bit, he put himself inside of me and it was different from the other time. It was gentle and kind and it felt like love. I felt loved for the first time in my life. When he released himself, I whispered in his ear, "I love you." I had no idea that was going to come out of my mouth and knowing it was way too soon, I had no idea what the response was going to be, but he said, "Ditto".

He dressed himself and then put my pants on and then my bra. His touch on my back made me want him more. The way I feel confirms how I do love him, no matter how fast it is. He put my turtleneck on and my sweater over my head and kissed me gently. He even put my boots on and tied them as if he was my servant and boy he served me well.

We both stood up, my knees were wobbly and he held my arms. He reached down for the blanket and saw a candy bar laying there…a Kudo and we started singing the commercial. "Kudos, I am yours, I am yours." It was perfect timing and quite fitting for the exchanges we just had.

I didn't want this night to end and I knew that Nate and Noelle were gone for the weekend so we had both places to ourselves. It was much easier at his fraternity; there was no sneaking in or out or a housemother on site. While we were walking to car, hand in hand, I had to ask, "What are we doing next?" "Getting something to eat and going back to my place where there is something that still needs to be done," he winked. I can't even imagine what he has in mind and I shutter thinking about it.

He pulled into the Pizza place to grab a pizza. I waited in the car. I was watching him through the window; he was so confident and larger than life to me. He is much more than I ever had dreamed of, and as of tonight, I was his. Life was good. He got back in the car and placed the hot pizza on my lap and we were off to his room. We were ravenous after our sex fest under the weeping willow and the pizza smelled fantastic.

Jonathon grabbed the pizza and I grabbed the duffle bag and followed him up the stairs to his room. We passed a few of his frat brothers in the hall and I could hear those muttering things about him being with me again. Thinking to myself and blinded by being in his presence, I couldn't understand what the big deal was. Do frat boys have girlfriends? I let it go and went in his room where we sat and ate pizza and laughed some more, as usual.

After eating, I shyly asked if I could borrow one of his t-shirts. I had to get out of this hot turtleneck and sweater and be comfortable. He handed me a Navy t-shirt, which smelled of him. It was totally turning me on. He took my boots off for me and then my pants, slipped my turtleneck and sweater over my head, and replaced it with his t-shirt. His t-shirt smelled of his cologne and his sweet scent, it made me feel warm and belonging.

He then took his clothes off and put some boxers on, as he seldom wore underwear. It was incredibly sexy to me. We were comfortable, we had full stomachs and it was a perfect time to just be and appreciate the newness of this whole thing.

There was no television in his room, just a stereo, so not a lot to do. He put a CD in the stereo of Van Morrison and I laid down on the waterbed, feeling exhausted but satisfied. I wanted him next to me. I pulled him under the loft and he lay next to me, stroking my hair until I fell asleep in his arms. A short while later, I was woken up by something burning hot. For a minute, I thought I had peed because of the waterbed but I didn't, thank god. It was the gel we never used Under the Weeping Willow. He didn't lie when he said there was one more thing we had to do tonight.

This fire was sizzling my nipples. The intensity was like nothing I could have imagined. He gave me some on my hand so I could apply to him. As I rubbed it on him he moaned. It was so hot, almost like burning embers on your body, no pain, just pleasure. He put his hot, hard penis in me and the tingling sensation was unbearable. He pulled in and out and then rubbed some on my swollen wet spot and that was it for me. I came and I asked him to go harder. He flipped me over and he entered from behind, pinching my fired nipples and pounding in and out of me until he could hold off no more and he came. The intensity of the heat and the force exhausted us. We both held each other until we could catch our breath.

"How'd you like that," he asked. "Pretty hot and amazing," I answered and we fell asleep in each other's arms for the night. We woke up the same way we fell asleep, his arms around me and my head on his chest; it was as if we didn't move all night. It was blissful but morning came all too quick. Jonathon leaned on his elbows and said he had to ask me something. Listening, he said, "I would love for you to come home with me for Thanksgiving." I paused and anxiety filled my brain with the thought of meeting his family. I had never been home to meet a guy's family before. I had already known Josh's family because we were friends before we got involved. "Are you going to answer me, will you come with me or not Brooke?"

The insecurities came out to him and I asked, "Do you think your parents will approve of me?" "Brooke, without a doubt. How could they not? You are the kindest girl I have ever met." "I would love to go home with you for Thanksgiving then. I'll let my mom know that I won't be coming home," I say, trying not to appear as excited as I was. "Then it's final, you will meet my parents and my best friend Rick." "Sounds like a plan, but I'm just letting you know, I'm nervous!" He tried to calm my nerves and was successful.

I rustled my way out of the waterbed and got dressed to go home and take a hot shower or maybe a cold shower after the night I had. I thanked him for the invite and told him I was looking forward to meeting his family. He smiled and said, "They will love you, as I do." He kissed my nose and I left.

When I got to my dorm, I called my mom and told her I was going home with Jonathon. She was happy for me and told me to be careful. I assured her he was different from Josh. She hated Josh for how he treated me. She was reassured. I was nervous and excited at the same time. I can't deny that I felt special for the first time in my life.

We were leaving on Wednesday to go to his parent's house and I won't be seeing him until then as we both had catching up to do with schoolwork. Monday night Jon called me. We chatted for a few minutes. As we were hanging up, without even thinking, the words just came out, "I really do love you Jonathon," and he replied, "Ditto." It was a cute thing to say but I wished I had heard the real words back because no guy has ever said those words to me. In time I guess, I hope.

Tuesday came and I was at classes all day and Pam and I had plants to hang out. Every time I heard the phone ring in the hall I jumped but it was never for me. Waiting and hoping for the phone to ring and hear Jonathon's voice, the phone never rang. We never discussed what time we'd be leaving on Wednesday, so I was in limbo. Pam and I did our nails and then played Boggle, which she was quite the competition. It was nice to hang out with her, but my mind was wandering and wondering why he hadn't called. Noelle was at the fraternity house but I was here. That bothered me. She was always there with Nate. She might as well move in. That was jealousy speaking. Why does she always get to be there and I have to wait to be invited? Maybe Jonathon had more schoolwork than Nate did, I don't know.

It was eleven am on Wednesday morning, the phone rang in the hall and I answered. It was Jonathon. "We're leaving in an hour and we have to take your car because mine still won't start." "Fine," I say irritated and I packed all my stuff together, ate a quick bowl of oodles of noodles and went to pick him up.

He was waiting on the front stoop for me with his duffle bag and his gentle eyes. I pulled up to the sidewalk and he had me move to the passenger's side so he could drive. I liked that he would drive, it made me think of my parents and their happy marriage. Oddly, I felt cared for and safe when the man drove.

We had a little over an hour drive to his house. This was the longest trip together so far, every other time in a car alone it has been minutes. The conversation was good, we had many laughs about the Hot Gel and it made me very horny. We got off the exit to take the back roads and he pulled me down on his penis. I wanted to please him in every way possible, so I stroked him and sucked him until he came. It was erotic in a car, while he was driving. I went back over to my seat and looked at his face as he looked content and seemed very proud of himself. I then felt proud I had pleased him. Only three days since we had seen each other and the desire was off the charts. It felt more like months.

Once he caught his breath and multi-tasked his zipper and the steering wheel, he smiled, "It isn't fair if I'm the only one in this car that is satisfied." "That's plenty okay, satisfaction is watching you come Jonathon," I said meaning it. He said he needed to touch me. His hand went up my skirt, pulled my thong aside, and caressed every part of me. Stopping and starting to make me crazy, all the while still driving. He found this funny. Finally, I couldn't take it anymore and held his hand there and I was shaking in my seat.

Who was this girl? This isn't me, I said to myself. I blew him while he was driving; let him rub me while still driving, not me at all. He has me swimming in unchartered waters but I love every minute of it. He loved me and me him that is what mattered.

We arrived at his parent's house and I was hoping they weren't home yet because I wanted to wash up so I didn't have to shake their hands with sex on mine. Thankfully, the house was empty. We washed up and he gave me the tour, showing me childhood photos and I made fun of his hair in the pictures. I would remember this moment forever.

He showed me his old bedroom and of course, he had an idea, but I said no. This isn't the time or the place and he let it be for now. Thankfully, he agreed because moments later we heard his mom yell, "Jonathon," and we came down the stairs. Mr. and Mrs. Sears held out their hand to me and I was so thankful that I had washed mine. We shook and exchanged friendly smiles. Clinging by Jon's side, I felt like the luckiest girl in the world. Mr. Sears asked Jon to help him grab some wood from the porch so they could light a fire. It was Mrs. Sears and I alone in the kitchen. She asked me where I was from, what my studies were and how long I have known Jonathon.

I was fine with the questions until it got around to the one about how long we had known each other. I told her a couple months. I continued to say what an amazing son she had and she replied, "I am surprised, he's never brought a girl home to meet us. You must be something special." I smiled back. Thankfully, they came back in with the wood and I followed Jon into the family room and helped him build the fire.

Still tense and not knowing how his parents felt about me yet, I went in the kitchen and asked his mom if she needed help getting ready for Thanksgiving dinner tomorrow. She said sure, so she handed me the turnip and carrots to peel and she began to whip up some pies. Chocolate Cream, Banana Cream and Lemon Meringue. I can never make Meringue so I watched her diligently. It came out perfect. I sliced up the turnip and carrots and put them in a pot ready to cook and mash in the morning. That was all she had for me to do. It was nice. We talked and she taught me the proper way to make Meringue.

Jonathon and his dad were sitting by the fire and having a nice conversation when I walked in the room. Jon pulled me on his lap and I was blushing. I was embarrassed that he did that in front of his dad. His dad said to both of us, "You two look really happy, it's a pleasantry to see." I smiled and Jon gave me a peck on my forehead.

After Mrs. Sears came in from the kitchen, finished with her pies, we played cards for a bit. We played no peek and it was nice. I was able to see how Jon's parents were very affectionate toward one another and it made me warm inside. This had to be where he got his sensual side from, his parents; they were obviously still in love after all these years.

It was getting late and we had to get up early for the Turkey Game at Jon's old High School. Mrs. Sears showed me to my room and Jon went into his. I undressed and put on his Navy t-shirt to sleep in. I wished I was in his room, but that wasn't proper at this first meeting. I got into the twin bed and thought about where I was and what this all meant. Does he really love me? Can it be possible? We were good together; we both had a wacky sense of humor and some of the same ideas about life.

He wanted to be an Engineer and me, a Lawyer for children, two great professions that would blend. Sleep isn't coming easy, I'm in a strange place and the man I want is in the next room, so close, but untouchable. It amazed me how when I was in his presence I didn't want anything but his body against mine. After a good hour or so, I heard his parents go to bed. The house was silent, and I could only hear my breathing, which was getting rapid while thinking of Jonathon right next door.

I rolled over on my side, away from the door, without hearing a thing; Jon walked in and got in bed with me. "No, we can't, your parents are here," I whispered. He tried to coerce me but I refused. Not in his parents' house while they were home at least. With a bratty look on his face, he pulled me out of bed and said, "Then come on. I can't know that you're in the next room over and not touch you." I gave in and followed him.

We tip toed down the stairs and he shut off the burglar alarm so it wouldn't go off when he opened the back door to the deck. It was cold. All I had on was his Navy t-shirt and he boxers with smiley faces on them. Thankfully, there was no snow yet but it sure was chili. He picked me up and carried me on the deck; he didn't want my feet to get cold. He placed me on top of the woodpile and he hungrily took my underwear off. His cock was sticking straight out of the flap in his boxers. I grabbed it and gave him a hand job while he was rubbing my wetness. He has his mouth on my clit and a finger up my ass. No words can describe how this felt; I grabbed his cock harder and told him I needed him now.

It was cold out and the moon was shining directly over us and he knew we had to make this quick. Both hungry for it! I'm ready for him to enter. He entered me. The way he thrust so hard in me, it was near violent. He was rough and distant, it was cold, and his demeanor was strange. It was as though this was the last time he would ever be with me; he seemed desperate and needed to hurt me.

Once he was done, we went back in the house and tip toed back up the stairs. He didn't even kiss me goodnight. He went into his room and shut the door. Getting back into bed, my head was spinning and my crotch was throbbing from the intensity and force that he used on me. In a strange way, I felt dirty. It wasn't because I was on a woodpile, I felt like I was just literally fucked.

After a sleepless night, I had to wake up to go to the football game. As my eyes opened, they were heavy and I felt like I was in a daze. Jon came in and told me it was time to have breakfast before we went to the game. I told him I would be right down. I looked at myself in the mirror and wondered if his parents would look at me as I felt. Like a used, dirty slut.

Entering the kitchen, the greetings were friendly. They asked how I slept and I lied and said well. In front of me were pancakes, bacon and a glass of orange juice. I ate what my stomach could force down and helped with the dishes after. Jon was helping bring some more wood in for the day and after that, it was time to go to the football game.

We were meeting his friend Rick at the game, a long time childhood friend of Jon's. I think I was more nervous about meeting him than I was his parents. After parking the car and scouting out for Rick in the bleachers, we found him. He was a handsome dude with dirty blonde hair and he looked like a body builder with not an ounce of fat on him.

Jonathon introduced us and we both gave a smile. I sat down on the bleachers and the boys stood watching the game. They hadn't seen each other in a long while; I wasn't getting in the way of that. The two guys were like schoolchildren. They were patting each other on the back, laughing, and reminiscing of when they went to high school at this school and played football on this same team. It was very cute to watch and see how they both had such a bond to one another.

Then I heard Rick say, "Hey do you remember that cheerleader you fucked right on these bleachers after the Friday night game against the Rockets?" Jonathon stopped in his tracks and looked back at me to see if I was paying any attention to them. I put my head down and acted clueless. "Yeah man, she was so hot then and she gave the best blow job." Hearing this, I needed to get out of there and get some air. I asked where the women's room was and told them I had to go to the bathroom. Jonathon didn't want me to go alone but I insisted he stay with Rick and finish his conversation.

"So Jon, what's up with bringing a girl home, that's not your MO? Aren't you just a love and leave-em or are you whipped?" "Rick, I'm fucked is what I am. Brooke has got me like I've never been before. I got it bad man." "She's smoking hot Jon! Is she good in the sack," Rick says trying to get all the details. "She's beautiful and the other part is none of your business, but in a word, incredible."

Rick was shocked at Jon's admission. These guys have played the field together for years and never did he think Jon would settle in for one girl.

I followed the signs to the women's room; got in there, looked in the mirror and again I saw that dirtiness I felt earlier this morning. What changed with him? Was it that I told him I loved him or was it that I agreed to be his? Clearly, I won't find the answers in my own head. I went back to the bleachers where they were now sitting down and left the middle seat open for me.

I sat down in between Rick and Jon. Rick started talking to me, "Brooke, Jon really likes you." "Really," I said. Hmmm, surprised he said that but it made me feel a bit better. "He's got it bad for you girl; I've never seen him like this." "Thanks Rick, it's nice to know I'm not the only one that has it bad," I laughed. Everyone has a past and I wasn't empty of that. I had Josh after all before Jon. He's no longer with the cheerleader so obviously, it's not worth my worry.

The game was over, it's time to head back to his parent's house to eat Turkey, Stuffing, Turnip and Carrots, Pearl Onions, Mashed Potatoes, and the wonderful pies Mrs. Sears made. At the dinner table, it was just his parents and the two of us. His two brothers and sister were at their in laws. Jonathon was the youngest in his family as well.

We said grace and we all started passing the food around. The meal was delicious and I had to save room for pie, Banana Cream Pie, my favorite. The conversation flowed and they were asking Jon about his plans for the rest of the school year and after graduation. He wanted to continue with school for his Masters and I thought that was great as I would be in law school as well.

Mrs. Sears brought out the pies and Jonathon took a piece of Chocolate Cream Pie, put it in his mouth, and turned to me with his tongue covered in the cream. It was cute, very cute in front of his parents, but it turned me on. I than took a piece of the Banana Cream Pie and started licking the cream off of my fingers. I then put my hand under the table, in his lap to find him hard. It was an insatiable desire I had for him.

I laughed at him because he was stuck at the table with a hard on. He wasn't moving until he shrunk back down. I helped clear the table and he started a conversation with his dad so he didn't have to move. When we were finished with the dishes, Jonathon, now being able to move, got up to say we had to get back to school. He didn't want to drive in the dark and I was only thinking that if it were dark, he might have a harder time finding my crotch. I chuckled. I think he really just wanted to get out and get to sex.

We said our good-byes and Jonathon and his mom had a long hug. He was her baby and I'm not quite sure she liked the idea of sharing him with me. Just a feeling I got from her. I hope in time it will go away.

Whew, it was over and we were alone again. I asked if we could just not fool around and just listen to the music. I had a lot of processing to do. Was I ready to hear about his past lovers, was I able to accept them for what they were, past lovers? I hope so, but I craved this guy and more importantly, I loved him and I didn't want there to be anyone else, EVER.

"Thanks for coming to meet my parents and Rick. Rick really liked you." "Thanks for having me, it was fun." Then he winked at me, just his expressions made me throb, everything about him, his eyes, his nose, his lips and his goddamn laugh, I loved it. His laugh made everyone laugh too. I was thrilled that I could make him laugh too. I loved hearing him laugh at my jokes or remarks, as stupid as so many were with me, but it was just one more thing I loved about him.

Approaching the last five miles until we got to his fraternity, I thought it was a good time to say thank you to him for everything so far. "Jonathon, you are like a dream come true, when we're not together, I ache." He smiled a smile, but a half smile. A tear came to the corner of his eye. "What's wrong?"

"Brooke, I don't deserve you." "Why did you say that Jonathon? You have been nothing but amazing to me and you have taught me so much already," responding confused. It made me sad that he didn't think he deserved me. I think he does.

The conversation ended because we got to the fraternity and we had to unload the car. There weren't many people back from Thanksgiving yet. Some of the frat brothers went home but some stayed so the house wasn't completely empty. Nate and Noelle were at her house. I was happy they wouldn't be there. I didn't want to hear Noelle and her sex noises.

Jonathon had to check some things out in the house and he told me to go ahead up to his room. I grabbed the duffle bag from him, walked up to his room, and turned the light on. On the edge of the loft, centered in the middle was a trophy. I had never seen this trophy before and it wasn't a sports trophy, it had a Hog on top of it. Whose was it and why did they win a hog trophy? I placed it down from where I grabbed it from and went to sit on the couch. While sitting on the couch, I noticed a piece of paper on the floor.

This read:

Jonathon, this trophy is presented to you for fucking the biggest Hog at the party Tuesday night. Congratulations! Oink Oink!

Thinking back, was I with him Tuesday night. No, Pam and I did our nails and played boggle and he never called. Oh my god, he fucked her! He fucked a fat fuck. The air is literally stuck in my throat and I can't breathe. I knew something was amiss when he didn't call. He cheated on me, right before he took me to meet his parents.

It's apparent to me now that I'm his but he's not mine. One way! I'm always in a one-way relationship. My heart skipped about five beats and I had to write him a note before he came in the room. He should be a few minutes still checking the frat house out. Not even able to think straight, I just started writing. My hands are shaking.

Dear Jonathon,
Congratulations on your trophy, it's a great accomplishment. You should be very proud. What an honor it must be to fuck the fattest girl at the party. I guess that's why you never called on Tuesday night

because it seems like you had your hands quite full.

You're a son of a bitch! The way you pounded me on your parent's porch. I knew there was something so raw about it and desperate. You fucking knew you were going to get this repulsive trophy and you wanted to fuck me hard because you knew it could be the last time. Why did you bring me to your parent's? You made a fool out of me? Don't call me or come near me. Oh and you were right, you don't deserve me you asshole.

I'm not yours,
Brooke

Tears are pouring down my face and my throat feels as if it is closing; thank god, I have my car. I drove to the neighboring college where my friend Sarah went and banged on her door. Looking as if I just saw someone murdered, she let me in. Her boyfriend was there and they were watching a movie. She had a TV in her dorm room unlike Asshole but he didn't need a TV, he had enough entertainment.

Sarah tried to console me and wipe my tears but nothing made me feel better. My heart feels as if it was just ripped from my body. I had no idea what to do. I still love this guy. I still wanted him in every way, but how could I? He was a fraud or just a complete player that preyed on the innocence to make himself feel better. Well, he sure knows his shit; I fell for it, hook, line and sinker and then some. What a fool I am. "Brooke, this isn't your fault and he was right, he doesn't deserve you, you're better than that," Sarah spilled. In my warped head, part of me felt badly for him. I honestly didn't know how to feel.

I knew I had fallen fast and hard and I truly loved

him. I had to have him. I've never felt this way before. I have an ache over my body when we aren't together. Just the sight of him and his voice made me feel wanted. Some things never change. I'm beyond stupid and naive, my original thought was obviously right. Why would someone like him want an average girl like me?

I stayed the night with Sarah; I needed to be with someone I trusted. She sat up and waited for me to fall asleep. She was the best friend anyone could ask for. She put a glass of water next to the bed for me and when I woke up; I drank it all, dehydrated from crying all night.

I walked down the hall to the bathroom, peeked in the mirror and my eyes were nearly swollen shut. Looking back at myself in the mirror, it reminded me of all the things Josh had done to me. Jonathon was no different, just like any other guy looking for a fuck. My face was evidence of the pain and more so of the obvious fact that nobody can be faithful to me.

I walked back to Sarah's room, got my things, and went back to my dorm. I was hungry but I couldn't eat, my belly was sick. I am ashamed of myself for letting my guard down. Stupid me, I allowed myself to believe he cared about me. Great sex doesn't mean it's love or even like. I'm a fucking idiot.

I heard the phone ring out in the hall and I let it ring. Someone else can get it. I was hoping it was my mom but it was Jonathon. I told the girl to tell him I wasn't here and she did. I couldn't stay here, I had to get out and be in my own surroundings. I packed a few things and I walked down stairs to sign out. I'm going home. I forgot my backpack, so I ran back upstairs to get it; I had some papers to do while I was at home.

When I opened the door to my room, there was a yellow piece of paper on the floor that I hadn't seen before.

I picked it up; it was folded with my name on it. What is this? It was a note from Jonathon. He's obviously been here and slid it under my door.

Dear Brooke,

Please forgive me!! I told you there were things about me I wasn't proud of. It meant nothing to me and its part of the whole fraternity thing. I didn't mean to hurt you, but it was my turn. I knew my turn was coming up before I met you and I probably should have told them no or met you later. I know this probably doesn't make any sense, but it is part of the whole code of the fraternity.

I need to talk to you. I need to see you. I need you. Kudos, Jonathon

I read the note and ripped it up in tiny pieces, threw it on the floor, grabbed my backpack and walked out. Got into my car and drove toward the highway. Passing the street of his fraternity, I was tempted to pull in but my intelligence kicked in and I kept on going.

Every song on the radio that played couldn't have been more fitting. Why is that? It's as if the dj knows when people are hurting. It was hard to drive as the tears wouldn't stop and the pit in my stomach was getting worse just by thinking about the trophy.

He chose the code of the fraternity over what we had together. That was the fact, the sick and twisted fact of that matter. Me, I was just someone to pass the time with until it was his turn. Everything he said to me was a lie! It had to be; otherwise he never would've fucked the fat girl. In my mind, love trumps all. Maybe that's why he never said the words. He'd feel guilty and that's only if he has a conscience at all.

Was the night under the Weeping Willow tree in the park nothing to him? He poured his heart out to me. The night at my dorm laughing and being close with no sex, what was that? Why did he bring me home for Thanksgiving to meet his parents? Was this all some kind of sick game? I know I'm no relationship expert, but I have a hard time believing he faked the connection we had. There is no way anyone could fake the passion, desire and magnetism we had. If he did, he was the best actor because I honestly felt loved. I guess this is how my life will be. Me giving of myself and receiving nothing true in return. All the feelings of unworthiness of love have rushed back to me and I feel like a complete fool. Why am I not loveable? Why am I always used and tossed aside when something else comes along? Maybe I'm too nice, too caring, but one thing is for sure, I didn't fucking deserve this.

Pulling into my mom's driveway at home, I sat and wiped my eyes before I went in. I didn't want to talk about it with her. I knew what she'd say and I didn't feel like hearing it. Mom didn't know I was coming home, so she was surprised to see me walk in the door. "Brooke, what brings you home? Are you alright, you look like hell," mom questioned. "Mom, I just needed to have quiet and no distractions to do my papers."

I wish I had called first so she could've made me a pot of soup; I haven't eaten since we got back from his parent's house. I asked mom if she would make me a pot of soup while I went up to take a shower, a long hot shower. Trying desperately to wash the pain away and thinking about the note Jonathon left me. It was so cold and meaningless. Thoughts of his touch, his lips, his gentleness and his need to please me, my mind is racing. Then thoughts to the woodpile, his roughness and distance, it all made more sense to me now. Why did he want to hurt me when he was the one that did wrong? This is fucked up.

Trying to clear my mind and put Jonathon out of it, I dried off, got dressed, went downstairs, sat in front of the fire, and opened my backpack. The soup was cooking and I hoped it would make me feel much better. Coincidentally, one of the briefs I had to write was for a divorce case where the husband had multiple infidelities. Maybe I should write my essay on the court system instead, right now, I thought. That's what I did.

My mom brought me a bowl of soup and it warmed my heart and my soul. It was the best soup, the cure-all for everything, hangovers, colds, flues and now a broken heart. Suddenly, there was a knock at the door. Mom told me to answer it was probably the paperboy coming to collect. My hair still wrapped in my towel, I opened the door and without looking, I waved and called out, "Come in, I'll get the money."

The voice went through my body like an electrical current. It could only be one voice, Jonathon's. "Hi Brooke, can we talk? I need to explain." I turned around and my mouth dropped to the floor. How dare he wear that fucking black turtleneck! Of course he looks beautiful as ever with a stuffed animal in one hand and a Kudo in the other. What was he a sadist; did he have a need to rip my heart over all over again?

"Brooke, we need to talk," he pleaded. I wondered how he knew where I lived. Who told him? He drove all the way here to talk to me. My heart sank and thought, well maybe he truly did care and the fat chick was really nothing. Weakened by his presence, I agreed to talk to him. It couldn't here, we had to go somewhere private. I yelled to my mom and told her I would be back in a while.

Down the street from my house was a park. I took him there. Nobody was there because it was November and it was too cold to be playing on the swings. "Noelle gave me directions and I had to see you. I can't sleep, I can't eat without knowing we are okay. Brooke please."

"I guess you should've thought about that before working on earning your trophy," I said with tear in my eye. He put his head down in shame, grabbed my hand into his, and held it tight. I pulled away; I was trying to be strong.

Even how hurt I was, just his touch made me hot and tingly. He kept saying he was sorry and it meant nothing. The words didn't make it better, I told him. He brought my face up to look into his beautiful eyes. I looked into his eyes with my bloodshot and puffy eyes. He opened his mouth and said, "I am so sorry I hurt you, it wasn't supposed to be like this."

"What the hell does that mean," I asked.

"Brooke you weren't supposed to be like you. You were supposed to be like all the others, but you're different."

"Are you saying to me, you fucking the fat chick is my fault?" He was silent.

All the others, huh, how many were there? I knew about the girl from his hometown that he fucked on the bleachers and of course the fat chick, but just how many others were there before me?

"I told you there were things I wasn't proud of Brooke, but I want to be different with you."

I turned my head away in disgust and I felt the urge to run. I opened the car door and ran into the woods.

He was calling my name and I wasn't turning back. He chased me, caught up to me, grabbed me, and kissed me hard. I tried to refrain but I just couldn't resist him. He stopped for a moment and stared at me, "Brooke, I love you! Please give me a second chance. I know I fucked up but without you, I feel like I am empty and my soul mate is gone."

Now feeling very dizzy after what I just heard, I didn't know what to do or say. The only thing I knew was this guy had a hold over me like no other. I did love him. I wanted him and I really did need him. This is crazy, god I know but I love him.

He kissed me again and I fell to my knees sobbing and wanting him like never before. I needed him to show me he loved me. He had to prove himself to me, with kindness, passion and love. I needed to feel it in my heart and my body. On my knees in the leaves, he came down to my level. He held my hand and kissed the tip of my nose, which made me tear up. I loved that. The simple gesture that made me feel special.

"I want to make love to you. I have to show you it is real," he whispered softly.

I was his; there was no denying that. He had me despite fucking the fat chick. I couldn't stop him; I wanted him in every way. The cold damp wood was where it had to be. I couldn't hold back another second. His breath was hot on mine and his eyes were watered up, as if he were to shed a tear. I was happy to see the tears in his eyes; he should hurt as much as I do.

He picked me up and hugged me so tight, like he was never going to let go. I didn't want him to. He stood me against a huge tree with little to no leaves left on it. He kissed me with that desperate force again and I responded with as much force as he was giving. The insatiable hunger. It had to be satisfied.

I put my hands under his turtleneck and rubbed his nipples until they were hard, then I put my mouth over them and he was hard pressing against me. This hunger is undeniable; it's now a need for both of us, not just me. He needed me too. He turned my body and put his body against the tree. He lifted me up and I wrapped my legs around him as he put himself inside me. He was holding me so tight, and his kiss was nearing barbaric. It was passionate. He gave a hard thrust and came inside of me. He then let the tears flow. He didn't put me down right away. He stayed inside and I could feel him soften, but I didn't want him to leave me just yet either.

"I am so sorry Brooke! I love you and I know you love me. Please forgive me," he desperately pleaded.

"Jonathon, I love you and what we have is intense. I know you feel it too, but I can't share you. You can't do this to me again, to us again."

"Brooke, look at me. It meant nothing and I know it was wrong and I hated it and myself after. I will never do this to you again."

Jonathon swore to me that this wasn't going to happen again. He said I made him want to be a better person and he was going to do just that. I agreed that I would forgive him, but I would have a hard time forgetting. It was going to be a work in progress for both of us. I loved him so much, too much probably. I felt I had little choice but to forgive him and see if we could move forward from this. He told me I wouldn't regret it.

We headed back to my mom's house; she was shocked when I walked in the door with a guy. I introduced her to Jonathon and told her he surprised me with a visit. "Nice to meet you, come on in and make yourself comfortable," mom said. Thankfully, my dad was out of town for work, he would've been able to tell that something was amiss. He always could and he hadn't always been a faithful man either.

He had a few affairs on my mom over the 30 years of marriage but mom always gave him another chance. My mom loved him since Junior High School and could never imagine herself with anyone else. She turned a blind eye at times to save their marriage. For us kids too, she didn't want to seem like a failure. Although, we all knew he had cheated and resented him for it, but they seemed to be good now, so we adjusted.

"Jonathon would you like some soup," mom asked. "Sure, Mrs. Walsh, that would be great." He ate down the soup by the fire next to me and it was as if he hadn't eaten in weeks. He loved it and felt at home at my house. This was where he wanted to be. Jon and I were very tired from the emotional day we had thus far and fell asleep on the floor next to the fire in each other's arms.

A couple hours later, mom had cooked dinner and asked us to come to the table. She made steak, baked potatoes and peas, her favorite meal. We joined her at the table; she asked Jon lots of questions. He told my mom about the childhood stories I had shared and we all laughed. Mom began to embarrass me and tell him how kooky I've always been. She became serious for a moment and gave him the MOM warning. "Jonathon, Brooke has had her heart broken before. She is an amazing young woman and not because she is my daughter. She will treat you like a king, she will do anything for you and she will make you feel like you are all that matters. Please do not hurt her, she is my baby," mom babbled on.

Jonathon looked at me, took a deep breath, "I don't intend to hurt her. She is incredible and I can say from the bottom of my heart, I love her." I couldn't believe my ears; he told my mom he loves me. Mom smiled, "That's great because you two look fantastic together and you really seem to have a strong connection." He reached over and kissed me on the cheek.

This went well and I knew that I couldn't tell my mom why he was here and about the fat chick. It would break her heart too and I don't think we need any more hurt. We cleaned up after dinner and my mom asked Jonathon if he was going back to school tonight and I interrupted and asked if he could stay the night, mom said yes. I wasn't ready to have him leave;

I needed more time to become confident in his feelings.

Mom told him he could sleep in my brother's old room and then said, "Well that's useless. I know you'll sneak in to his room Brooke, so as long as there is no hanky panky, that's okay with me." We both smiled at each other and said no problem. Meanwhile, I knew this was a challenge that he had to fight with all of his might. It was a good challenge; it's nice to leave him wanting. This was going to be a great night.

We both headed on upstairs to my room, still with posters of cats on the wall and my large stuffed animal collection placed neatly on my bed. I had forgotten about this and I was a bit embarrassed that I still had stuffed animals. He walked in and smiled and said, "This little bear I brought you will go great with the others; it will make them have a new friend." We both laughed. I told him, "No way! This bear will be coming back to school with me and when I'm not with you I will sleep with it."

He was obviously confident that I'd forgive him because he ran out to his car and got a duffle bag. Not his car, his roommates. His car still didn't work and he didn't have the money to fix it as a college student. While he went to the car, I took out his Navy t-shirt and put it on. Still unwashed from all the times I've worn it because I didn't want his smell to go away. Juvenile, I know, but that was me, a pure romantic.

He came back in my room, saw me with his shirt on, came over and kissed me. "I'm so glad that you brought that with you. It makes me feel so much better." I turned the TV on and we got into bed to watch an old rerun of Happy Days. I told him he was like the Fonz and we both laughed.

Everything seemed normal again and I was happy. He tried to get in my pants but I wouldn't let him. I reminded him of the promise we made to my mom. "Come on Brooke, we'll be quiet. She'll never know."

"Nope, a promise is a promise; you'll have to control yourself."

I knew he was getting frustrated as I could feel his hard on against my leg and I wouldn't give in. He surely got an A for effort. Too bad there was no way that I was going to risk anything on the first night he met my mom. I was laughing at him and he was less than pleased, but he owed me to say the least. He was going to have to suck it up, which he did. We finally fell asleep. When I woke up in the middle of the night, I thought he was gone. I felt the other side of the bed and there was nobody there. I jumped out of bed and looked in the bathroom and he wasn't there. I went downstairs and found him on the couch writing me a note.

"What are you doing," I asked him? "I'm writing you a note. I couldn't sleep and I had to put my mind to rest. Go back to bed and I'll be up in a few minutes. I really need to finish this."

I agreed and of course, couldn't get back to sleep out of curiosity and fear of what he was writing. Maybe he changed his mind. Maybe I'm just a convenience fuck after all. He came back in the room and curled up next to me.

"Jonathon, what does the note say," I asked nervously. "You can find out when you read it. You can read it now or later, Brooke; it's all up to you."

Hell, I'm not waiting! I ran down the stairs and grabbed the note from the counter and wrapped a blanket around me and began reading:

Dear Brooke,

I couldn't sleep. I sat up and watched you sleep for a while, you are so adorable and you looked so peaceful and precious. Watching you sleep and seeing the beauty that you are made of made me want to write to you.

What I did was unforgiveable. Because of who you are, you have forgiven me and I am grateful. I never really had a relationship before like this. You and I fit together. We make each other laugh, we both have great career paths ahead of us, but you make me feel like I'm not missing anything. I always felt there was something missing in my life until now.

When I read the note you left me after seeing the Trophy, I wanted to die. For the first time in my life, I didn't think I could go on. I actually moved my room to another room because I couldn't stand to be in there with the reminder of you and the wrong I had done in that room. I'm now in the front of the building; it's a much bigger room with windows. We can see the street from the room and we can now watch all the drunken people walking home.

The night at my parent's house, I was desperate; I needed to feel you as deep as I could because I knew there was a chance you were going to find out. I had to know that I gave you the most pleasure. Selfish, I know but it was how I felt. I'm twisted.

The thought of you being with someone else makes me sick and ache all over. I can't imagine not being with you and seeing that smile and hearing your moans from our lovemaking. I never want to lose you and I will try to be to you what you deserve.

Truly sorry, Kudos, I am yours.
Jonathon

Tears are welling up in my eyes after reading his note. I sat back and asked myself, "Can I trust him? Does he really mean all of this or is this his way to remain in control?" I don't know. I think we should head on back to school in the morning and see how things play out. Time will tell. I hope the hell he means it because I can't imagine my life without him.

The slightest thought of not being with him really makes me sick all over. My body is actually getting numb just thinking about it. I really hope this time will be the last of his screw-ups.

The sun burst through the blinds and woke me up. I was still on the couch and Jonathon was still in my bed. I heard some noises from upstairs, then it and dawned on me my cat is probably locked in my room. I went upstairs and opened my door quietly, not to wake Jon and sure enough the cat was in there and I let her out. I stood over the bed and watched Jon's stomach go up and down. He had his arms wrapped around one of my stuffed animals and he looked like a little boy.

Looking at him now I can't imagine him ever being unfaithful, he is angelic looking. One thing that watching him made me think of was trust. I think he screwed up and everyone does. I'm going to take a chance and trust him again. I leaned over and gave him a kiss on his forehead and he started to stir. I didn't want to wake him so I turned around and quietly started walking out of the room. He called out, "Come here, you."

"I'm sorry I woke you," I whispered. He pulled me to him and just held me tight. It was warm and reassuring and my doubt about trusting him melted away. I told him we should think about getting on the road to go back to school; we already missed one day of classes. Neither one of us showered, we just got our things together and said good-bye and thanks to my mom. She packed me up some leftover soup and I was so excited because I could actually heat it up in my microwave. The simple things in life always make me the happiest.

My mom loved that I chose a school closer to home. My sister Kate was in Arizona, my brother Rob who moved to his wife's home state of Georgia and Joan who moved to Vermont with her husband where she taught 5th grade. I was all that she had left close by. She loved when I came home because she was often alone with my dad traveling for work.

Jonathon followed me to the highway and we followed each other for most of the way until I thought I saw him get off an exit. Assuming he needed to go to the bathroom, I pulled off the exit. He was stopped on the side of the road waiting for me. I pulled up behind him and he got out of his car and came to mine. He gave me a kiss and said, "I love you so much," he got back in his car, and drove ahead of me. That was so sweet, first take home soup and an impromptu kiss, I love the simple things.

I passed him on the highway and gave him a gesture that I knew would make him crazy. I laughed all the way to our exit. He pulled up beside me and returned the gesture. He rolled his window down and yelled, "I'm going to take a shower, come over when you're done and see the new room." "That sounds good," I smiled, "See you soon," and I blew him a kiss and tooted my horn as I drove past his street.

Walking into my dorm that bitch Steph was outside her dorm staring at me. What's her problem? She yelled across the street, "How's Jonathon?" I yelled back, "Great, thanks." I could feel her eyes on me while walking to the door, so I turned around and waved. She really bugs me.

Inside, I went to sign in and the housemother told me I had a package. She gave me the package and it had no return label. Excited, thinking it was from Jon; I hurried up to my room and ripped it open. It was a small box with a stuffed hog in it, no note, nothing. Running to the bathroom to puke, I hugged the bowl and cried and cried, puked some more. Who sent this to me, the asshole? Will I ever be able to forget?

Someone is obviously not happy about Jon and me but I don't know whom. I will find out. Right now I have to take a shower. Today is a new beginning for Jon and me with his new room and no visions of that Hog Trophy. In the shower, I shaved my legs and thought; I wonder if he'll like this, so I took the razor and shaved my private. It was so infant- like, clean and refreshing.

I put a pair of jeans on and a sweater and braided my hair in a French braid and then grabbed the stuffed hog and went out the door. Walking to my car, I noticed that my tire was flat. I went inside and got Pam to help me and to see if I ran over something….it was slashed. What the fuck? I hadn't been in the dorm for an hour yet. How could someone do this without being seen? I know Steph did it. What is her major malfunction? I marched over to her dorm and asked for her to come down and see me. That tall Amazon girl came down the stairs and smirked at me. I asked her, "Did you slash my tire?" She rudely responded, "No, why would I do that?"

"I don't know why you would. Why are you always talking about me or asking about Jonathon?"

"I just think you guys make a cute couple," she said with a smirk I wanted to remove from her face. "Cut the shit," I sneered.

I gave up and turned around to walk back into my dorm to call Jon. I dialed the number and he was the one that actually answered the phone. I told him about the flat tire and he had to come pick me up. A few minutes later he was in the driveway. As I was getting in the car I looked up to the dorm across the street and saw Steph staring out the window at us and I gave her the finger.

We drove off and went to his fraternity. We walked into his fraternity house and went right to his new room. It was a much nicer room. It's bigger and brighter with the two windows in front. The waterbeds separated this time by a nightstand with an alarm clock and a boom box on it. I rather liked the curtain that separated the beds before, but this was okay. There was actually a real sitting area so you didn't just have the bed to sit on or a tiny couch; there was a long couch and two chairs. It was nice.

In my right hand I had the box with me, he asked, "What did you bring me?" I threw it at him, "Open it up and find out." He opened it and his faced got flush, "What the fuck is this Brooke?"

"You tell me! It was sent to me with no name and

no return address." He immediately dropped it, pulled me to him to hug me. "Brooke, I am so sorry. I'll find out who sent this. I'm so sorry, you don't deserve this."

"Let's burn it," I said. We got some matches from the drawer, lit it on fire, and threw it out the front window. "Good-bye hog."

Jonathon was wearing Obsession for men and that scent made me crazy, its light sweetness appealed to me and I liked that he was wearing it. He was wearing a pair of thick brown cords, a cream pullover sweater on and he was stunning. I couldn't help myself and I pulled down his zipper, nearly catching his pubic hair in the zipper, as he had no underwear on. He was now peaking right out at me. The perfect size and texture, everything about his body was perfect. His ass was soft and supple and his chest was built and his legs were long and not with a lot of hair on them. His shoulders were broad and muscular and his hands were like a multi-functional tool, he was more than ambidextrous.

He threw me down on the bed. With his teeth, he undid the zipper to my jeans and pulled them down with his mouth. My underwear was already wet. He makes me so wet. With his tongue, he rolled my underwear down my legs and kept them around my ankles. He licked my legs, kissed, and rubbed my thighs and I tried to move, but I couldn't because my ankles were tied. "Don't move, I owe you," he said.

He opened his mouth and breathed his hot breath on my vagina, blowing on it and lightly grazing it with his lips. He is teasing me and taunting me. "I'm going to make you suffer like you made me at your mom's house," he said. He got up, took my jeans off the floor, and tied them around my hands. He was in complete control and I was his for the licking.

He went down to my toes and sucked each one, one at a time. I'm so close to exploding; but he was going to make me wait. I kept pleading to him and he just laughed. He worked his way back up to my vagina and realized I had shaven; all of it. This turned him on even more and made him feel, touch and kiss every crease and crevasse of me. "Brooke, you are so soft and smooth. I want to make you come, but not yet," he smirked.

He was teasing me and as much as I wanted him inside me, I liked it just the same. He licked my clit like a lollipop, moaning and enjoying himself; he stopped again and went up to my breasts. He teased them too and my lower half was now burning, wet and hotter than with that gel we used before.

"Please Jonathon, don't stop! I need you now," I pleaded. He laughed again. Back down to my lower half and he started over again, he added one finger, putting it in, taking it out. I really can't control myself. He added another finger and his tongue and he then took his perfect penis, rubbed it up and down on me, and stopped. It was torture. "I told you, I want you to suffer and I'm going to make you beg," he said with a sexy smile. He went back to my clit and he finally let me release, "That's my girl, you are all mine!"

He then entered me and pulled out, re-entered and pulled out, he is punishing me. I couldn't do anything about it as he has my feet and my hands out of the equation. He was in complete control and loving it. Finally, he stayed inside me and got faster and harder with each thrust. I was actually seeing a star, that's how hard he was fucking me. He let out a big moan and filled me with his hot cream.

"Don't ever make me wait for you again Brooke. I needed you and you made me suffer, so I owed you a payback."

"I will remember that Jonathon." After we settled down, I put my clothes on and asked him to the do the same. I needed to talk to him about what was going on. He must know something about the package I received and the slashed tire.

"Jonathon, we need to talk about the package and my tire that was slashed. This has to do with you; why else would someone send me a stuffed hog? I really don't want to know who the girl was that helped you achieve the trophy, but I would like someone to speak to her, not you, you've had enough contact with her. If this is her doing, she needs to stop now. It seems obvious to me that someone doesn't want us together. Do you have any idea why or who that would be?" With a panicked look in his eyes, "Maybe someone is jealous of you." "Oh no, I don't think that's it Jonathon. Maybe somebody wants you and that's why they're doing this to me. Slashing my tire means that I couldn't go to you; so it has to be someone close to me that knows what I'm doing."

"Please just tell me this, does the Hog you fucked live in my dorm?" I was afraid of the answer. "No," he said. "Do I know her Jonathon?"

"I don't know if you do. Can we just put this

behind us? I don't like talking about it. I know that I hurt you and it makes me sick that I did." "Jonathon, you do your research and promise me you will tell me if you find out who it is."

He pinky swore me. I got up and went to walk out to go to the bathroom, and he held me back. "Brooke, you are all of who I want, you are the only one, those days are over for me, you are mine and I am yours," he confessed. "Well, I hope that's true because I don't want to share you with anyone, not a fucking hog or anyone else for that matter."

After returning from the bathroom, there was something else I wanted to talk to him about…. Christmas. "Jonathon, Christmas is huge in my family. We have a big party on Christmas Eve and I was wondering if you would like to spend Christmas with my family and me," I asked nervously.

He hesitated for a second, "There is no place I would rather be than with you on Christmas. Does that mean that I won't be able to have you while we are there?"

Laughing, I say, "I think we can find a way. We may just have to be creative." This turned him on. He threw me to the floor and ripped my clothes back off and his as well and got on top of me and slowly entered me once again, it was nice and not rough this time. He was loving, kind and I felt so connected and united with him.

"Brooke, I love you! You and I are one and that's how I intend it to stay." He kissed me softly and I held him and wouldn't let go. He went in and out of me and let loose. He tickled my arm and then made me swear to him that I trusted him, which I did. He wanted me to tell him again, that I was his and only his, which I did.

It seemed strange to me that he was the one that needed the reassurance. A very complex guy. He was so powerful in his presence; yet needed to know repeatedly that I was his. I was proud to be his. I was happy and I loved being with him and laughing. Making love to him was pure perfection. I would be his forever, I assured him.

"No more sex tonight Jon; I'm sore. Can we just be together?" "It's your fault, you make me insatiable, but I'll try my best." "Be a good boy now, let's just hang out."

A knock on the door scared us both. Jon went and answered it; it was his friend from down the hall. He gave him a package that came for him while he was gone. "Hey man, I would've brought this to you earlier, but it seemed as though you were busy," the guy said. Jon took the package from him and thanked him and he went on his way.

"What is it, what is it?" I laughed like a little girl. He had no idea who it was from; so he opened it and put it right back in the box and told me it was nothing. "No way, you aren't hiding it from me! What's in it Jonathon?" He didn't want me to see the contents so I grabbed the box from him and opened it myself.

In the box were four clear bags full of different kinds of condoms. Two bags were French Ticklers, one bag was Red, White and Blue and the fourth bags were multicolored condoms. "What the fuck is this all about? Do you plan to fuck until your dick falls off Jon? Did you order these? We don't even use condoms; what do you need these for?"

It was as if someone had pressed the mute button, he couldn't speak. "Well… I'm waiting!" "Brooke, I have no idea who these are from and I didn't order them," he said stumbling on his words. "So, someone sends you a box of condoms, one thousand at least and for no particular reason? What are you not telling me? I'm sure these aren't to put in the bathrooms here. This box is addressed to you Jon. Why," I demanded. "I don't know, for Christ Sakes. I have no idea who this is from and why," he shouted and was getting angry, but fuck him.

"In a day's time, I got a stuffed hog sent to me, my tire slashed and you got a huge box of fucking condoms. That is about all the surprises I can handle in one day. I'm exhausted. I'm going to sleep in Nate's bed since he's not coming back until the morning. Jonathon didn't say a word.

I got up on Nate's bed and Jonathon on his and we were silent; you could hear a pin drop. My mind is going in a million directions and I don't know what to think. Let me just fall asleep, wake up, and have these gifts be just a nightmare. Finally, I heard noises and they were coming from Jonathon. It sounded as though he was talking to himself along with sniffles. What is this guy or who is he? So many secrets it seems, yet I can't get enough of him. I'm as fucked up as he is.

I woke up in the morning in Nate's bed and Jon had left for class. I heard the alarm clock go off but I was mush from the day before and didn't get up with him. Finally, I got myself out of the bed and put my jeans and shirt on and saw the box sitting there on the floor,

I kicked it over and left.

Forgetting I didn't have a car; I walked to my dorm. It was freezing but I had to have some space and time to figure this entire thing out. I got to my street and I saw Noelle walking to class, which was a rarity in itself. She stopped to talk to me and I asked her about the Hog Award and the box of condoms. She laughed her ass off and told me she would talk to me when she got out of class. What was so damn funny about this? Did I miss the joke? I wasn't laughing.

I got back to my room and was grateful there were no more packages for me. I got in the shower and all I could smell was sex from yesterday, for an instant, it made me feel sick. What was this guy hiding? Who is he really? Does he really love me? I know I love him but do I really know him? The doubts came crashing into me as I wait for Noelle's return from school.

She knows something; I can feel it. Twirling my thumbs until she got back from class, luckily for me it was her short class of coloring; she was a fashion design major. She was good at coloring, so this suited her just fine. I was getting madder by the second at her for laughing at what I told her. I started thinking about things she has said to me since Jon and I got together. She definitely knew something and she was going to tell me when she walked through that door whether she liked it or not.

Finally, Noelle walked in. I was taking this opportunity to get the truth from her. "Noelle, put your things down and sit. What are you hiding from me? What do you know about Jon that I don't?"

"C'mon Brooke, I told you he's hot, didn't I and you like him right. What is the problem," Noelle whined? "There is a problem Noelle; someone sent me a fucking stuffed animal after he got the hog award for fucking the fattest girl at the party. Did you know about that?" She laughed again. "What the hell is so goddamn funny," I questioned her.

"Oh my god, you should've seen her. She was huge," Noelle ridiculing. I now shouted, "You knew about this and didn't tell me or try and stop him?" "Hey, he's a big boy. He makes his own decisions. It was hysterical. That girl was in heaven with him on top of her," Noelle went on with pure joy. "I'm going to throw up! What else do you know," I asked?

Not sure I wanted to know. "Brooke, Jonathon is a male slut, he fucks anything." "So, he must be like you huh," not being able to hold back. Now who is laughing? "Yeah he is, but even worse," Noelle grinned. "How could you not have told me this? Why would you set me up with someone like that?" "You need to loosen up and get laid once in a while, I figured he was perfect for you," she said with a snot ass smile.

"You call yourself a friend? With friends like you I surely don't need enemies, and it's clear that I have some!"

"I'm sure you have many now that Jon has been with you for this long. I'm sure there's a line of girls that would like to beat the shit out of you; they were all just one night fucks. All I can say to you Brooke is, from what Nate has told me, Jonathon never repeats his lays. He's been with you more than anyone before, so I would say you must be pretty damn good if he is sticking around you. Maybe your fucking sweetness and your holier than fucking thou attitude is changing him, but you always wanted to change the bad guys, didn't you? Too bad it failed with Josh; don't you remember?" Noelle snickered.

"Did it ever occur to you that Jon may really care about me Noelle? He told me he loved me, you know," I proudly told her. Shocked, Noelle didn't know what to say, "Well, then I'm happy for you. You're a lucky girl to go to bed with him on a regular basis, he looks like he's incredible in the sac. Not to mention the moans from the girls he produces."

Trying to contain myself from punching her in the face, I walked out of the room and walked back to Jon's fraternity. I knew he was out of class; he had some big time explaining to do. Rehearsing in my head what I'm going to say to him when I entered his room on the walk over. Going over it in my mind, changing things as I walk just knowing by the time I get there nothing of my plan will come out the way I want it to.

Walking up the steps to his fraternity, my stomach is in knots. I hear him laughing in the hall with the guys. A laugh that is completely distinctive and one thing I love about him. He noticed me coming down the hall then left the guys, and went in his room. The guys are standing there unfriendly, as usual. I shut the door behind myself and Nate and Jonathon are in the room. Nate, so sweet and kind, says hello and asks if we need time alone and I told him no. Anything I have to say can be said in front of him. He stayed and Jon asked, "What's up?" "Jonathon, I just had a nice conversation with Noelle and she told me you are the male slut of this place." Nate piped in with defense, "Brooke, he's not like that anymore since he met you. Nobody can believe it; he's different and that's because he cares about you." "This is true Brooke. I told you I've done things I'm not proud of, but I am faithful now."

After a long conversation with Jonathon and Nate; with Nate trying to convince me that Jon was like this before he met me and things are different now. I with a heavy heart decided to trust him. It sure does explain a lot to me why girls are upset with me. Obviously, if they needed or wanted to get laid, they knew Jon was always willing; he didn't have a preference in size or looks.

Trying to push this out of my mind, I headed to the mall with Pam to go Christmas shopping. Thinking about what Jonathon may want or need being a college student was tough, but then I walked by this beautiful long woolen grey coat. It would be perfect for him to go on interviews with the added plus he would look great wearing it. Thankfully, I saved up from English tutoring because this wasn't a cheap gift. I know he'll love it and I was so excited. It'll be gift wrapped and ready for Christmas Day with him.

Pam and I ate at the food court and I decided I would confide in her about what has been happening. "Pam, I want to tell you some things." "It's no secret Brooke, you're in love, and I know it. You're glowing, just mentioning his name you light up. Please don't be mad at me, but he's damn hot," she laughed.

"I know he's hot and I'm not mad at you for saying that. Pam, things have happened and I don't know what to do. The sex is electrifying; he makes me feel a tingle just by looking at me. He brings me to complete ecstasy, but before we met he slept around …a lot."

"Hey, he's a college boy and if he had no commitment with anyone that shouldn't affect you. It's obvious he likes you; just take it step by step," Pam says logically. I trusted Pam; she was my best friend on campus and while she was saying this, all I could think about was Jon. I needed him and I had to show him I trusted him. "Pam, I have to go to him. I'm sorry."

"Brooke, go get your man and I'll pick out your gift now," she said pushing me out the door. Running to the car, I literally felt weak in the knees and excited that Pam gave her approval. The mere thought of Jon on top of me was making me crazy; this car can't drive fast enough.

I parked in front of his building and ran up to his room; he was actually taking a nap. I walked in quietly, took my clothes off and snuck in next to him. He was snoozing and this was my time to give him some pleasure. He of course was naked already. Good thing he slept that way most times. I didn't have to wake him to get him unclothed.

I took his foot in hand and started to massage it and give it little kisses. I went up to his calf, then I caressed his thighs and he was beginning to get hard. I took him in my hand and sucked his balls and then his cock. Slowly licking it and sucking it until he was fully awake. "Well hello there," he said smiling.

He then pulled me to him and he kissed my nipples and then my mouth. This kiss was heavenly, soft, tender, tongue on tongue; it was enough to make me explode. He pulled me under him and entered me, ready and willing. No need for lubrication; this guy was my natural lubricant. In and out, he thrusts himself and it was beautiful. This was love, true love making. He is irresistible! He's made me insatiable as well. I can't get enough of him, when he comes; it's a gift to me. To know that I can pleasure him and to hear his moans and pant-like noises, it's arousal on its own.

"That was awesome. You are so beautiful Brooke. I thought I was in a dream but it was better than any dream. It was you in the flesh. Thank you for being mine." I kissed his nose and promised, "Always!"

Snuggling after making love, I couldn't contain myself; I had to tell him I bought his present. He was like a little kid wanting hints, but I wouldn't give in. He told me that he already had my present as well. I started to ask for hints and he wasn't giving any either. It was joyous. Still naked, he realized that he hadn't touched me. That was fine by me; I didn't need to come every time. Being with him was enough for me but he has to know he's pleased me. He began going lower down my body and touched me ever so gently and he captivated me with his stare. He wanted to watch my face as I reached orgasm. Circling around and rubbing me, I lost my breath and collapsed underneath him. Holy shit! He was proud that he could turn me on so much and give me an orgasm. It was an accomplishment for him. However, I wasn't complaining.

It was time to leave and go back to my dorm. I have requested a single room and it should be ready by tonight. Pam and I are going to move my things to the new room. Just the thought of being Noelle's roommate anymore makes me sick, even though she is never there. I need my space. It'll be awesome to wake up in my own room, with privacy and not her sorry ass gloating and being in my business.

Kissing Jon good-bye, I ordered him to "Behave."
He promised he would and said, "Kudos!" I smiled
and left to go see my new room. Noelle wasn't home.
Thank God, it was hard enough to do this and it's
much easier when she's not there. I 'm running up the
stairs to go by where the new room was. I was excited
to see a sign outside of the door with Brooke Walsh on
it. It's ready and so am I. Pam came running down the
hall yelling to me, "You have to go inside!" "What's
the matter is it gross," saying with fear in my voice.
"No, just go inside." She was acting as if she just got a
new puppy or something, she was so cute and a great
friend. "Should I be scared?" "No, I will tell you this,
you will be in shock, but in a good way. Brooke, this
is a new start for you here in many ways, you'll see
when you open the door," Pam speaks in a soothing
voice. "You're really scaring me now Pam!" "Just
open the door Brooke!"

I opened the door; all my things were in the room.
Candles lighted the room and there were kudos spread
all over the bed and yellow roses on the desk with a
card that said:

Dear Brooke:

*Welcome to your new room. Our New Room. I hope
you like how I set it up. It was such a great day! One
of the best, other than the day I met you. Smelling your
clothes as I moved them from your closet and drawers,*

your smell was arousing me. I had a hard on almost the whole time. I want you to know, you make me happy and I truly love you. I cannot imagine my life without you and I never want to! You have changed me. Look under your pillow. Enjoy your new room, our new room and remember I love you. Yours Jon

"Pam, did you know about this," trying to speak as the tears are pouring down my face. I can't believe this. It's beautiful." "Yes, I knew about it but Noelle was the one that let him in the room." "Hmmm, she just must be happy to get rid of me. Pam, can you give me a minute so I can look under the pillow, god only knows what he put under there." "Sure, I'll be back in a bit with some treats." Lifting up the pillow, I was shocked with what I found. It was a picture frame with a childhood photo of me and a childhood photo of him and a picture of each of us as we are now. A caption added read:

"Let's never forget our childhood, but become one as adults...Jonathon"

Oh my god, this is the most beautiful thing I have ever seen. He is for real. I know longer have any doubts. I hung the picture on the wall in front of my bed so I could see it every night before I fell asleep. What an amazing day. If this was the gift he had talked about, I don't need anything else.

Pam came back in with some beers and cheese wiz in a can and crackers and we hung out on the floor playing Yahtzee and had fits of laughter. Pam was such a good friend and I loved hanging with her. She was normal and nice and we laughed so much together, except when she sang, which made me cry at times. She has a beautiful voice that bellows from her feet. I just love her.

It was after 11:00 when there was a knock on my new door. "Come on in," I shouted. I looked up and saw him, his dark brown hair and dark eyes and his smile that looked like he just walked out of a magazine. I ran into his arms and wrapped my legs around his waist kissing him and kissing him and thanking him. "This is my exit. Good job Jonathon! You made her very happy," Pam said then gave him thumbs up.

Still legs and arms wrapped around him, he carried me to the window to look at the moon. It was full and beautiful and he turned to me and said, "I love you Brooke Walsh. I don't know when, why or how you did this to me, but you did." Smiling through the new tears, I told him, "You made me the happiest girl tonight and I knew I loved you from the first time I saw you."

He carried me away from the window and put me on the bed. He looked up, saw the picture frame in front of the bed, and smiled. He lay down next to me and he hugged me as if he would never let go. His breathing became heavier and mine synchronized with his. No sex, just hugging and it was perfect. We fell asleep together like that, fully clothed and wrapped up like a pretzel. It was the best sleep I ever had, in our new room.

The hustle and bustle of the Christmas holiday has started. I've been packing to go home for the Holiday and excited that I get to spend it with Jonathon and my family, this is perfect to me. Jonathon is getting his things together and we're heading home today. Looking around my room, my heart is full and happy when I see the pile of Kudos stacked up from Jon spreading them all over my room on that move in night. The excitement is killing me and I can't wait until we leave.

As I pack the car, I see Steph across the street. She's staring at me. I walked up to her and asked, "Do you have a problem?" "Yes, why do you get to have Jonathon," she squawked. Stepping back and opening my mouth, "What business of it is yours?" "Brooke, I had him before you and I've known him longer than you." My reply is simple, "Steph, I don't know why things didn't work out for the two of you; I can't say I am sorry though, but I'm not the one to give you the answers. Steph, what I can tell you is this, we are in love and committed. It obviously wasn't meant to be with you and he and you may have to move on. I'm sorry you are having such a hard time understanding this. Merry Christmas Steph, I have nothing else to say to you." Steph walked away mumbling under her breath. She just doesn't get it; she and Jon are not going anywhere.

That was not what I needed at this time. Now I see that it explains why she's always staring at me and talking about me. He was with her. The Amazon that she is, he fucked her and she is obsessed with him! This is not a good combination. Steph will not ruin my holiday with him. I won't let her.

I shut the trunk to my car and waved good-bye to the girls at the dorm and drove away to pick up Jon. My mind is reeling as I drive, but I have to accept that he had a past before me and he is different now.

Pulling up to his fraternity, he's on the sidewalk with all of his bags and he's smiling and seems very happy. He put his things in the trunk and had me move to the passenger's side so he could drive. Such a guy thing that I just love. I didn't want to spoil our ride or our time away from this crazy campus but I had to let him know about Steph.

We drove away and I waited until we got on the highway and told him that Steph and I had a conversation. Immediately, his demeanor and expression changed. He asked, "What about?" "You. She was outside staring at me and I went over to her and asked if she had a problem," I said. Jon's eyes grew wider and to my surprise said, "You did, she can kick your ass." "Yes, I know she can but I'm sick of her gazing at me and whispering when I'm around. She's upset because you're not with her and you're with me." He laughed, "She is nothing like you and she was a one- nighter, maybe a two- nighter and I have no interest in her that way."

"She is obsessed with you Jon." "I know. I've heard and I think she's the one that sent the hog, slashed your tire and sent me the condoms," Jon admitted. "Really?" "She's a good friend of one of my friends from back home that goes to school here. She had us get together, since then she's been at every party and stalking me. A big mistake I made after way too many beers," speaking with shame. "It sounds like you had a lot of those," I said, very sarcastically. "So, there is nothing between you? Is she just jealous and wants more from you, "I asked. "I promise you, there is nothing. I will make sure she stops. I'll talk to my friend and tell her to tell Steph to knock it off and move on."

"Okay, let's end this discussion. This is our time and I don't want to waste it talking about other girls. We're together now Jon. Your past is your past and that's where it should stay. I love you, despite your really bad decisions about screwing everyone."
"Thank you," he cleared his throat and put his hand on my knee, sending shivers through my body.

"Jon, I have to warn you, my mom will have you doing things to get ready for the party tonight, she doesn't care who it is, she'll make them work, so be prepared." "That's fine, but my work isn't free. You'll have to pay me for it," he said teasing, but serious.

"I will, I promise," smiling back at him.

"My brother Rob and his wife Shelly will be coming in tonight, probably right before the party starts. My sister Joan will be here with her husband Mike around the same time. My sister Kate flies in at 8 pm, so we're the only ones to do the dirty work. Lucky us, huh? It'll be fun though and it'll be good for my mom to see you slave away for her."

It's hard to be alone with him and not on top of him. I found myself staring at him as he was driving and my whole body went numb. He is definitely the love of my life. He's beautiful, funny, smart, charming, sexy and mysterious and I love all of him, flaws included. He caught me staring at him and asked, "What?" "Nothing, I just love you so much!" "I hope you love me even more after the surprise I am going to give you before we get to your mom's house," seductively speaking. So secretive he is. It undoubtedly turns me on. "A surprise? You know I don't like surprises Jonathon." "Babe, this is a good one. It's from my heart. It's something I want you to have." "Now you really have me anxious Jon." "Don't be, Brooke it's a good thing."

About a half hour left to home, we put Christmas Carols on the radio and were singing 'Rocking around the Christmas Tree', it was hysterical. "I'm going to rock you around the Christmas tree," he said making pelvic thrusts. "No you aren't! You know the rules!" "Brooke, don't you know rules were made to be broken?" "Yeah, some of them," I laughed.

Getting off the exit, "We're almost at your surprise. I can't wait," saying it like a little kid. He pulled into the park that we'd been to before. There were a few kids sledding, so he took me to the other side by the trees. He got out of the car and grabbed a box from the trunk, opened my door and brought me to this huge tree and had me stand with my back toward him and close my eyes. He took my coat off and I was freezing. It was December, what was he doing? He took my right arm and put it into a sleeve and then the left arm. He got me a coat too? That's what I was thinking. This wasn't just any coat; this was his coat. His Fraternity coat. This meant that we were a real couple.

I turned to him, not knowing what to say and I said nothing. I just grabbed his face and kissed him. He lifted me up and pulled my zipper down. He pulled his zipper down and slipped inside of me. Turning me up against the tree, he thrust harder and harder, it felt desperate again. I didn't like the feeling, so I asked him, "Why does it feel like you want to hurt me sometimes?" "Brooke, I'll never hurt you. I just need you so much and when I am inside you and going hard at you, I'm in complete control and I know you're all mine that's all I want."

"Sometimes I like it hard Jonathon, but other times

it makes me feel like just another one of your fucks."
"Is that what you think you are to me," he scowled.
"Sometimes I really do, I'm sorry," "Brooke, when I
go harder with you, it's that I can't get enough of you.
It's all about wanting and needing and loving you," he
explained. "Then harder is good, but not always," I
said.

The tree is beautifully decorated and I can see that
the cat has gotten into some of the ornaments. The
smell of pine and cinnamon, the roaring fire in the
family room and the living room, makes me so happy
to be home for the holidays. Mom is in the kitchen
making me a pot of soup and writing her *To Do List*
for us. My sisters and brother won't be here until the
party tonight, so they'll get out of doing mom's list.
Jon gave mom a kiss on the cheek and charmed his
way right to her in asking what he could do to help.
Mom loved a person willing to help; he just scored
some big points. Mom gladly gave Jon a list of things
to do and me as well. I couldn't start until I had soup,
so we sat and had soup and planned the evening out.

The piano was just tuned for my dad to play. We'll
all stand around tonight and sing the twelve days of
Christmas, which is a tradition in my family. Dad was
going to be home a bit later and he was going to to get
some food ready, he loves to cook. This is the first
time he'll meet Jonathon. I'm a little nervous, as I'm

the baby and he can be protective, I think he will love him as much as I do though.

Bellies are full from the soup and the bread that mom picked up from the bakery. It's time to work on that list and then transform ourselves for the party. Jonathon has his duties, I have mine and we are diligently working to get them done. All the while Christmas Carols are screaming through the house and the season is here, it is cheerful and warm.

One final touch and the house is ready. The food is simmering for the guests, the piano is ready, the lights are on and twinkling and it's time for a shower and to get dressed for the best family party of the year. Mom had to run out to the store for ice and I got into the shower.

The water is hot and I'm feeling so gitty and happy. Feeling so calm and blessed, I was living every girl's dream. As I turn to grab the shampoo, I feel a tall, wet body wrap around my back. "Jonathon, hey, we can't do this." "Your mom isn't home, it's okay," he informed me. He washed my back and kissed my neck, sending chills down my spine. I could feel his erection up against me.

He put my hands on the wall and put his hand on me, down there, the hot water, the hot wet hands, I was going to explode. He then entered me from behind and he was slow and gentle, in and out, wanting more, I grabbed behind me and pulled him harder into me. It was quick but delicious, he came and we washed each other and got out. "Hey, I thought you didn't like it hard," teasing me. I smirked and hit him with my towel. "But I love my dirty girl."

Jonathon came out of the room wearing pleated black pants, a red shirt and a green tie with snowmen on it. He looked so handsome. He was clean-shaven and his face was so smooth. His brown hair was shiny and perfectly combed. I had to feel if he had underwear on. "No underwear Jonathon?" He just smiled that sexy smile at me. "I love my dirty boy." We kissed and I turned back to get myself dressed.

I came out of the room into the hallway where Jonathon was waiting for me. Wearing a sleeveless black velvet dress with gold trim, above the knee and gold pumps with a 3 inch heal. "Brooke, you are so beautiful, I'm the luckiest man to have you as mine. You are staying right by my side tonight, I don't want anyone near you, you're all mine." "Don't be silly Jon, I'll be mingling and seeing people I haven't seen since last year and you'll be mingling as well. Besides, there will be some pretty ladies here tonight, trust me, and I trust you."

Walking down the stairs, I heard my dad come in. I took a deep breath, time for the introduction. I ran to him and gave him a big hug and he said, "My baby, how beautiful you look. It's so good to see you." Ignoring the beautiful creature next to me, he hugged me again. "Dad, this is Jonathon." "Nice to meet you Mr. Walsh, he shook his hand and said, "You're right, you have a beautiful daughter." "Yes, I would like her to stay that way, so don't break her heart," dad gave his warning. Jonathon assured him he had nothing to worry about and my dad told him to call him Ron. It went well, so far so good.

The doorbell rang and it was my brother Rob and his wife Shelly. They were expecting their first baby. Rob called out, "Hey Rookie!" Rookie was his nickname for me because I was the youngest. "Get over here and give your big brother a hug." I went and hugged him and he whispered in my ear, "is this him, damn I even think he's handsome." I turned and introduced him and Shelly to Jonathon.

Still in front of the door, it opened and Joan and Mike came in. Joan and I looked alike; she was just taller than I was. I introduced them to Jonathon and all I was waiting for was Kate to come in, we were the closest and I missed her terribly.

I left Jonathon to talk with my sister and see if anything else needed to be done before the house filled up. Rob and Jon went and grabbed a beer and were talking sports and laughing, they seem to hit it off well. Mike joined the guys and they looked like fast friends. Joan was more interested in how everything looked for the party, as she knew I was helping mom and she rarely gave me credit for anything. Mom was hovering over Shelly and rubbing her belly to see if the baby would kick, this was going to be the first grandchild, after all.

The doorbell rang and in came the first guests, all smiles and toting bottles of Eggnog and wine. Then came in Kate, I ran right up to her and hugged her almost knocking her over. I couldn't wait for her to meet Jonathon; I knew she would just love him. I interrupted the guys and introduced Kate to Jonathon and he told her he had heard many great things about her and they began to talk school, as they were only 6 months apart of graduation.

Within an hour the house was full, kids, and adults and of course, Santa came as well. Santa gave all the kids chocolate lollipops and listened to them rattle off their lists and addresses so he knew where to bring their presents. Jonathon went and sat on Santa's lap and asked him for one thing for Christmas. He wouldn't tell me what he asked for and Santa had to leave to get his reindeer fed and ready for the long night ahead.

Dad is on the piano, he's playing Jingle Bells, and taking requests, his playing was flawless, all by ear. A woman from the back of the room yelled, "It's time for the Twelve Days of Christmas!" So it began. Everyone grouped up and had a day to sing, it was tradition after all and Jon and I had Nine Ladies Dancing, which was appropriate for him.

The night went on until after 1:00 am and all the folks with kids had gone and got them to bed so Santa could come. It was a magical night. I turned to Jonathon and asked him, "What did you ask Santa for?" and he replied, "You." That's so sweet but you already have me." We grabbed hands and fell asleep in front of the dwindling fire.

Rob, Mike, Joan and Kate helped mom and dad cleaned up while Shelly fell asleep on the couch and Jon and I on the floor. My mom was in her glory with all of her kids' home and sharing this Christmas Eve together. They were all sleeping at a hotel tonight, even Kate so Jon could have a room. There was always at least one drunk person who couldn't drive home and needed a place to sleep. Kate loved her sleep and didn't want to be awakened by a blubbering drunk.

The morning came too fast, at first thought, but it was Christmas morning; I can give Jon his gift now. Not so fast though, I have to wait for mom and dad to wake up and then we can start. Christmas always makes me feel so young and excited. It's never been about the gifts for me, it's about seeing what you have given to others, their reactions, their smile and their love, that's what truly matters to me.

Mom and Dad made it down the stairs, hung-over and needing coffee, which I had brewed a fresh pot for them. To them it was indeed their first gift. Claude was the one who stayed in the extra room and he snuck out before anyone was awake. Jonathon had lit the fire and brought wood in to keep feeding it. It was snowing out on this Christmas Day, we have snow and it is beautiful. The fire is roaring, mom, dad together, the love of my life Jonathon, and I, together on this very special holiday, things couldn't be better.

Mom gave me a gift and began, "Brooke, this will help you through anything, treasure this and always remember, you deserve only the best." I took it from her hand and ripped the paper off it. It was a book; the cover on it had a rainbow and blue sky on it. I opened it and there was a note from mom on the first page, the rest of the pages were empty, this was a journal.

Mom wrote:

Dear Brooke:

You are my baby girl, no matter how old you are, you will always be my baby girl. On these blank pages, I want you to write anything that comes to your mind. Write when you are happy, when you are sad, your experiences, your successes and your failures. This book is yours. It is private and it is for you to express yourself without any opinions about it. I love you Brooke, I hope these pages get filled with only joyful things, because that would be the best gift you could give me, I always want you to be happy, loved and healthy.
Merry Christmas,

Mom

"A journal mom, this is the best gift you could've given me. I love it and I sure hope that there are only happy things that are entered into it too. I have no doubt that they will be as long as Jon and I are together. Thank you Mom, I love you."

We exchanged gifts for a while and I wanted to give Jonathon his gift. He was excited. I told him to grab the big long box from under the tree. He looked like such a little kid, he slowly ripped each side of the paper and opened the box and pulled out the long wool coat. He stood up and put it on and I was so pleased at how well it fit and damn, how hot he was. He loved the coat and said he had never had anything of his own that was so nice; he usually had to borrow a coat from his dad if he had to go somewhere nice.

"It's your turn, Brooke," Jonathon got up, he grabbed a great big box from under the tree and handed it to me. It was light as a feather and wrapped in red paper. I opened the top and there was another wrapped box inside, opened that, found a smaller wrapped box inside, than came to the bottom and it was a tiny wrapped box but wrapped in gold. I took the wrapping off, opened the black velvet box, and found an exquisitely dainty pearl ring. It was precious, I began to cry and he said to me, in front of my parents, "I got you a pearl because it symbolizes purity and innocence and I love that about you. You are my pearl." My mom and dad were about as shocked as I. I gave him a kiss and he put it on my finger, "I will treasure this forever Jonathon."

After, we cleaned up all the wrapping paper we had breakfast. Mom made crepes with strawberries and cream, my favorite. Of course, Jonathon had ideas for the whipped cream, but he had to refrain. It was fun watching his mind reeling and his desire for me as strong as mine for him. I enjoyed watching him squirm.

My mom and dad were going to be heading over to their friend's house and Jon and I were going to hang out and take a nap before we met them there later. Mom and dad will be making pork pies with their friends and play some cards before the crew got there for the evening dinner. We were to be alone, which felt like an eternity to wait.

We both showered, separately, and my parent's left. After we both showered, we went downstairs, I turned on the television, and "It's a Wonderful Life" was just starting. I'd never seen it before but Jon had mentioned that he and his parents watched it every year, so we sat down to watch it. Leaning back in his arms, this feeling of completeness and pure happiness encompassed me. There were no distractions, it was he and I and this movie. Twirling my hair in between his fingers made me feel safe and loved, just his touch was making me think of breaking the rules. We were alone. Nobody has to know and its Christmas after all, a day for giving.

The fire was crackling in the background, the voice of James Stewart playing and the two of us who were in need of one another's touch; all rules were gone, broken. Jon licked his finger and put it gently in my ear, which felt odd but erotic, I sat on top of him, he kissed my forehead, the tip of my nose and then his tongue entered my mouth. His tongue was like a soft magnet that I stuck to, tasting him and wanting more, all of him.

He picked me up, laid me in front of the fire, he then stood above me with his new coat on, and it was hysterical. I pulled him down to me, grabbed him under the coat, he then removed the coat. Our bodies were rubbing against each other's and the heat is burning, from the fire and the passion. Sweat is dripping down from his forehead into my mouth; he is exploring every crevasse of mine.

"Brooke, I want to memorize every inch of you. I want to touch every part of you." Breathless and no words forming, just want. He started at the top of my head and worked his way down to my fingers, sucking each one at a time, placing my fingers on myself and watching me touch myself. As he went down to my belly button, I was losing control. He met my hand and started to lick me, soft tongue strokes, while holding my hand there to play with myself while he licked. He went to my thighs, then behind my knees and kissed there and down to my toes.

"Now, I have felt every part of you. I can go to my favorite place; inside you. You're so wet and warm Brooke. I love being inside of you. I love you so much," he whispered. He entered me, kissed me, and then stopped. He pulled out of me, put my hand back on myself, put his hardness in between my breasts, and said, "I need to give you a pearl necklace to go with your pearl ring." I had no idea what that was. His penis thrust in between my breast, he came all of over them, and I came as well with the help from him. Sweat and cum flowing over my body and it was erotic, true lust and love. We took another shower and resumed the movie that we'd stopped watching to cure our hunger.

We both fell asleep. I woke up before him and grabbed my journal, first entry:

December 25:
Words really can't describe how I feel. Loved, wanted, lusted, cared for, belonging, forever, hot, sex, orgasm, these are just a few. I could not have asked for a better Christmas and I feel so lucky that Jonathon is in my life and he loves me. I know he really does. This is like nothing else I have ever had. I see myself with him forever. He has changed and I am so happy, he is sleeping next to me and he looks so peaceful. I could stare at him for hours. His mouth keeps moving and he is so handsome. How did I ever get so lucky to meet him? This is the best Christmas Ever! Until next time.

"Hey sleepy head, it's about time. You were snoring and I thought you were going to talk in your sleep. We have to get going to the party now. We slept for 3 hours," I said while nudging him. He grabbed me to him and kissed me with passion and conviction, "Thank you for everything, my coat, your body, all of you. I'll never forget this Brooke Walsh." "Neither will I, neither will I. This was the best Christmas I ever had."

Rob, Joan and Kate took me upstairs to have some time alone without Jonathon in earshot. He stayed downstairs with mom, dad, Shelly and Mike. I was a bit nervous on what they had to say. They all hated Josh and weren't shy about letting me know that. Rob was great at reading people, so I trusted him. Joan, she, no matter what was critical of Kate and me; she was very conservative and timid about relationships.

We all sat down on our parent's bed and Rob went first. "Rookie, what do you like about this guy," he asked. "There are so many things Rob, he makes me laugh, when I'm with him, I feel whole and comfortable and myself." "Are you going to marry this guy," asked Joan. "I would in a heartbeat if he asked." Kate joined in, "Are you using protection? I wouldn't want you to get pregnant while in college?" "Yes, Kate, we are," I assured her.

"So, what do you think of him," I asked Rob, Joan and Kate. They all said that they really liked him and that he seems very genuine. "He's very open and honest about his feeling towards you and we all liked that," Rob said, "I trust that he's good for my baby sister." Phew, they approved, we all hugged and went back to get ready to leave.

Saying good-bye to my parents before heading back to school was bittersweet. My dad always gets emotional and it makes me not want to leave. "Jonathon, it was great meeting you and having you here for the holiday. You obviously make my daughter very happy. Keep it that way or you will have to deal with me," dad said pointedly. "Dad stop! He makes me very happy and is good to me." "Mr. Walsh, I intend to continue to make her happy and I would be worried if I were her dad as well. She is precious," Jon was trying to reassure my over protective father.

Mom, of course packed me a box full of cookies and treats and a new Cross Pen to write in my journal, she is so sweet. Hugs to you all, "Happy New Year," we wished them and we got in the car and headed back to the campus. The snow was dwindling which was good for driving, it was so beautiful. Driving through the neighborhood, there were kids outside building snowmen and snow angels, it brought Jon and I back to our childhood.

We spent the ride talking about what we used to do as kids and how he used to white wash a kid that stole his bike in first grade. I told him about the time I was walking down the street with my best friend when my brother and his friends came out of nowhere and were bombarding me with snowballs and how I went inside crying. It was a perfect ending to a perfect week. Reality was before us though, classes starting up after the weekend and finals coming up.

Jon finally asked, "What did your family say about me?" "They all thought you were great and they never saw me look so happy. Mike wants you to go up to Vermont for a weekend to a football game. Rob said he trusted you, which means a great deal, as he's not trusting often, especially after my relationship with Josh. They all loved you, like I do." He was relieved and sighed, "I'm so happy they approved of me. I was nervous."

Jon was going home for the weekend for New Years to be with his family and I decided to stay at school and hang with Pam. He was bummed at first, but I thought it was good for him to have some alone time with his family, he didn't go home as often as I did. His mom didn't like me either so it was best I stay back.

He asked me if I would stay in his room while he was gone, just so he knew where I was and that I was close to him. I agreed and asked if Pam could come too and he said sure.

New Year's Eve was here and Pam and I decided it would be best if we went to Jon's room so we wouldn't have to drive. There was a huge party going on at this fraternity for New Years, but we stayed in the room, drank hot beer, and played around with an Ouija Board. It was freaky. At midnight, a knock came on the door and it was Tim, Jon's neighbor from across the hall, he said, "Jon's on the phone for you." "Thanks." I stumbling to the phone and so excited to hear his voice, "Hello." "Hey Brooke, Happy New Year! Are you being a good girl? Are you staying in the room?" "Yes Jonathon, I'm being a good girl and Happy New Year to you. I'm staying in your room, but there's something missing." "What's that," he asked. "You," I said loudly. "I'll be back tomorrow, don't miss me too much or I'll have to worry," he said with a reluctant tone. "Don't worry about anything Jon. I'm going to try and sleep without you in your bed. I guess Pam will have to do." "Better Pam than some guy," he stressed. "Jonathon, I told you; you never have to worry about that. I love you and that means everything," saying to him while annoyed. "Brooke, you better go to bed. I love you," he said and we hung up.

I got back to the room and told Pam I had to go to bed because Jonathon said so. We both laughed and Pam said she was going to go to the room down the hall and see a few friends. I got into bed and went to sleep. Thankfully, she didn't wake me when she came in. I woke up in the morning wrapped around her as if she was Jon. She was a great friend but she snored all night.

Later that night, Jon came back and I wanted him to be able to unpack and chat with his frat brothers before I went over. I waited until 9:00 and went over; he had a few beers with the guys and was a bit drunk. Regardless, I was happy to see him. He grabbed me by the hair when I walked down the hallway where he was. He brought me to his room and threw me down on the bed. "What are you doing," I yelled. "You fucking bitch made a fool out of me! You told me you loved me and that you weren't leaving my room last night," he cursed.

Confused and petrified of how he was acting, I asked him, "What the hell are you talking about?" "Don't play all innocent with me, you know what you did," he said with rage in his eyes. "No Jon, I have no idea what you're talking about. I sat here all night with Pam and played the Ouija Board. After you called and told me to go to bed, I did and Pam went down the hall… alone," I exclaimed.

"Get up you fucking liar! Get out of here," he yelled to me. Scared and still confused, I did and walked down the hall and got in front of the stairs and he ran up to me and said, "You will never make a fool of me again." Then he pushed me down the stairs and left me there. I was able to get up but I was hurt. I called Pam to come and take me to the hospital. I told her that I tripped over a hose they were using to fill the waterbeds and I fell down the stairs. She didn't ask me any other questions as she knew most of the guys did have waterbeds.

We got to the hospital, I had x-rays and nothing was broken, but my neck was sprained so they gave me a neck brace. It was humiliating at best. Went back to my dorm and locked myself in my room. I cried myself to sleep. Waking up every so often and wondering what was Jon talking about. Why hadn't he called me to see if I was okay?

I woke up in the morning very sore, my neck is stiff and this stupid neck collar is annoying the shit out of me. Noelle stopped me in the hall, and asked, "Are you okay? I heard what happened, those damn hoses, hah?" "Yes, they should be a bit more careful of their placement. I'm clumsy for sure. It was my fault. I was distracted and not looking," I told her, hoping she would believe me.

She asked me if I wanted to go to the movies with her tonight, shocked and unsure but I agreed. She was the closest person I had to home and I needed home right now. Wondering if he was going to call, I thought about not going and said screw him, he fucking pushed me down a flight of stairs, he deserves to call and not have me here. Noelle was actually doing me a favor.

On the way to the movies, I asked Noelle, "How was your Christmas?" "Christmas was good; I got a ton of clothes," she responded. "How come you aren't with Nate tonight," I asked. "Nate is with Jon tonight. They have some meeting to go to and then they're going to play pool. I'll head over later. Are you going over there later tonight," Noelle asked. "No, not tonight," I said. She questioned me why and I told her I had to get ready for a big project that was due soon. It was believable, as I always did my schoolwork. Surely not, like high school.

We went to the movies and saw Beaches. It was so sad and with what I had already gone through last night, I couldn't stop the tears from falling. It was exhausting. Noelle was actually crying too, which was surprising. She wasn't the sympathetic type. Noelle dropped me off at the dorm and headed to Nate's, aka, Jon's. I wanted to puke. I walked upstairs and there were three messages taped to my door from Jon. I took them off and ripped them up. Fuck him. The school project can wait; I'm heading to Sarah's and going to spend the night at her school. I'm so lucky she's nearby. She's the only one I can tell what really happened. I called her and she'll be waiting for me.

I drove over to her campus and ran up to her dorm, out of breath. She opened the door after my knock, took one look at me, and freaked out that I had a neck brace. "What the hell happened to you? Did he do this to you," she yelled. She knew me like no other. I couldn't lie to her. "Yes, but I don't think he meant to." Sarah was outraged that I was making excuses for him. "Jonathon thinks I did something and I have no idea what it is. I just know he was drinking and was very angry." "You aren't going back to him Brooke; he is no good." "I love him and he loves me, Sarah. This was all a misunderstanding." "Nobody throws someone down the stairs that they love," Sarah said. "He was drunk and upset about something that I supposedly did, it's my fault." "This isn't your fault Brooke, are you kidding me?" "Can we not talk about it anymore? I'm fine," I demanded.

She got the hint that I wasn't going to say anymore, so we went to her neighbor's party. She had plans already when I called but said she would wait for me. Her boyfriend was going to be there and I didn't want her to lose out because of me, so I tagged along. There were some other guy friends from home at that school too and at the same party. I chatted with them for a while and went back to Sarah's room while she stayed at the party.

Sarah always wanted to make sure everyone was okay and I assured her, I was, I just needed to be away from the people. She understood and I went and crawled into her bunk. My stomach feels empty, missing something, maybe this is how Jon said he felt before meeting me. Suddenly and stupidly, I'm missing him.

The tears pour down and I can't breathe. I need to know what he thinks I did. I need to know before I can let go. I'll have to talk to him that's all. I can't let him think I did something when I didn't. I can't let the love of my life go without hearing the allegations. I know everyone thinks I'm an idiot for staying with him. I know I am too but I love him so much.

Sarah came in after 3am and I was sleeping. She was tipsy and crawled in with me. That's what best friends are all about. She snored all night long and I didn't get much sleep after she snuggled up next to me. It didn't matter to me; just having her there for me was great. The morning came and I let Sarah sleep off the wine coolers she had last night and went back to my dorm.

Four more notes on my door that Jon called, plus an envelope. I opened the envelope; it was a letter from Jon.

Dear Brooke:

How do I begin? I'm so sorry for what I did to you. I never meant to do that. I was drunk and upset and I am so sorry. I feel like I lost my best friend. I can't sleep at night not knowing what you are doing and whom you are with. I don't want to lose you; I will

forgive you for what you did on New Year's Eve.
Will you forgive me? My heart is aching and I need
to see you I need to see that you're okay. Please come
to me, please, I'm begging you.

Kudos,
Jonathon

Sobbing as I can't believe what I'm reading. He'll
forgive me for what I did? I didn't think staying in his
room at his request with Pam all night was a fucking
crime. Maybe he thinks I contacted a hot dead guy
through the Ouija Board. What the fuck? I need to
know what's going on. I need to know what messed up
lies he's been told and stop it!

I ran to the bathroom to take a shower, get dressed,
and drive over to his fraternity. I wish he didn't live in
a goddamn fraternity. I banged right into him as I was
walking in the front door. I wasn't even looking at
where I was walking.

I looked up and saw his face, he immediately tried
to hug me as if all was great and I backed away from
him. "Jon, we need to talk. You obviously have some
information on me that you need to share."

"Can we go up to my room and talk," he asked,
hesitantly. I agreed and told him he couldn't touch
me. We walked into his room and it was a disgusting
mess. He hadn't cleaned a thing in days. Half-eaten
sandwiches and clothes all over the place, it was a
disgrace; even the flies were there to join us.

Not wasting anytime, I jumped right in to hear what
messed up thing he was going to accuse me of now.
"So, Jonathon... what is it that I did here on New
Year's Eve? Did I not flush the toilet right, or did I see

a man's reflection? Did I get too close to Pam? What are you accusing me of," I asked pissed off.

"Tim told me that you went to the party that was in his room. He said when he went downstairs for a beer, he came back and was told you were making out with Jeff," he informed me. "And you believed him? Who the fuck is Jeff? Thanks for your trust. For your information Jonathon, I left this room once, sorry twice to go to the bathroom and then to answer your call, that's it. Have you ever heard of innocent until proven guilty Jon? I would never do that to you and I certainly would not take the word of a guy that is probably pissed that you have a girlfriend," I yelled.

"Just who told Tim this information, Jonathon? Oh, let me guess, Amazon Steph was at the party. You're an asshole! She was the one and you believe what she says! Give me a break. I get pushed down the stairs because I supposedly made out with some guy Jeff; who I have no idea is and this is all because of her? Unbelievable Jon, this is classic. You have no right whatsoever to accuse me of anything when you have earned trophies for your actions," I cried out.

"I have to go! To think that I missed you and needed to see you; I'm the fool, not you," I lashed out. "Brooke wait, please don't go," he screamed down the hall. He looked like a lost puppy and I was enjoying it. I turned around and said, "If you don't want me to go, then you better come with me because I'm not staying in this frat house with these assholes that can't get over the fact that the male slut has a real girlfriend," I shouted.

He followed behind me and I told him to get in the car. I drove to my dorm and I took him by the hand and walked across the street. He was panicking; he knew what I was going to do. He and I were going to face Steph together for the last time. He begged me not to make him go there. "Why Jon? Will she be telling me some more of your little secrets?" "No, I just don't want you to get hurt," he replied. "I'm not worried about getting hurt, this is stopping tonight. I'm sick and tired of what this bitch is doing to me, to us!"

We went to the door and asked for Steph to come down. Surprisingly, she did. They told her that Jon was here and she was all wet in the panties about that. She must've been thinking it worked and that he came for her after all. No such luck Amazon! She turned white when she saw both of us there. We went outside, so I could spare her some embarrassment. I don't know why I care, but it was common courtesy, I guess.

"So Steph, what did you do on New Year's Eve," I asked. She paused for a second," I went to a party at the fraternity." "Oh, so did you see me there," I asked. "Ah Ah Uh", she stuttered. "Well, did you see me at the party," I asked losing patience. "Stephanie, was she at the fucking party or not," Jon snickered. "I didn't see her there; I heard she was in your room playing games like only a loser would do on New Year's Eve."

"Why would you ever make up a story that she was making out with Jeff and she was never even at the party," Jon asked filled with rage. "I don't know," she clammed up. "Yes you do and I'll tell you this right now, you and I will never be. You repulse me! You sucked in bed and furthermore, you smell like a rotten fish. If you ever so much as look at Brooke again you will deal with me. If you ever send another fucking package to her or me again, I will have you arrested. Do you understand me? Furthermore, Brooke is nothing like you, she isn't a cheater," he shouted with anger.

Her voice was shaking and she slithered out a soft, "Yes, I understand." "We're done here Brooke. I'm sorry I doubted you, I love you," Jonathon said loudly so Steph was sure to hear. Steph hearing that about put her on the ground.

What did he mean by calling her a cheater? What does he care if she is or not if she was a one-night stand? I'll have to ask him about this, but not now. Interesting.

Giving high fives across the street back to my dorm and our room, I felt invigorated; it was actually worth falling down the stairs to have had him defend me to that Amazon. The door closed behind us and Jon was ravenous. He attacked me like a barracuda. He pinned me up against the wall, grabbed my face, and looked straight into my eyes he said, "I'm so very sorry and I was wrong, so very wrong to mistrust you. My mind goes crazy when I think of anyone else touching you, I become someone else."

"Kiss me you asshole." He did more than that; he almost sucked the breath out of me. He tried to go down, but I stopped him. He had to suffer as I had. He put me down and walked over to where the picture of us used to hang and he began to cry. "Brooke, the thought of another guy being with you made me insane. I wasn't rational or fair and I can't stand to think of anyone else touching you. Brooke, my mind literally goes in circles of crazy even thinking about someone else's lips on you, or hands, it turns me into someone I've never known."

"As I told you before Jonathon, I'm yours and that means only yours which doesn't mean that when you are away I will play with others. I'm not like that and you should know that. I am committed to you. Trust is very important and you need to trust me, for Christ sakes. I've trusted you and you betrayed it already. You can never hurt me again; I will leave you and will never come back," I said desperate for him to understand.

He pleaded with me, "I will never touch you in a way that will hurt you again, ever, I swear. I've never felt so strong about another person in my life." "I hope you mean that because I will never forgive you if you do." I said making it very clear.

He thought that his emotions were enough to make me have sex. Wrong, he'll have to wait. "What happened to the picture Brooke? I hope you didn't throw it away." "No, I put it away after getting my frustrations out on it." I grabbed it from my desk drawer, broken glass and all and handed it to Jonathon. "I'll fix it," he muttered. "That would be great, seeing that you're the reason it's broken." "I'm sorry Brooke."

"Jon, I'm exhausted, it's been a very long week and I haven't slept much. Can we just go to bed?" "As long as I am next to you, I don't care what we do," he said. I changed my clothes, put some sweats on, and wouldn't let him take his pants off. Knowing my weakness and me with him, I would let him in. He was pouting. I had to be strong. I just laughed at him and he gave in. He finally lies down next to me and put his arms around me. I snuggled into his neck and fell into a peaceful sleep, finally.

I got up for class in the morning and I knew I couldn't avoid Steph as she was in my class. Wearing Jonathon's fraternity coat, I felt confident that she wouldn't approach me. However, this could throw her over the edge. Everyone knows what it means to wear a guy's fraternity jacket. She passed by me and gave me a half smile. I wanted to punch her, but she was worth shit to me and not worth my energy. We sat in class like adults and it seemed to be okay. I can only hope she got the hint and will leave us alone, time will tell.

After class I went back to my dorm to take a nap. Jon was still in my bed. I was so happy and horny and he suffered all night. Poor baby. He heard me come in and smiled at me and I went over to give him a kiss. He pulled me down on top of him and kissed me hard, I told him to fuck me, and he said, "No, I'm going to make love to you." He was so deep in me; I could feel him in my chest. He was slow and gentle and it was nice, but this time, I wanted it hard and fast and it wasn't happening. He had tears running down from his eyes as he moved deeper into me and I realized at that moment, he was sorry and he really loved me. He was truly hurting.

Finally, things seemed to be getting back to normal, or as normal as it can be on a college campus. I'm looking forward to our trip to Arizona to my sister Kate's graduation. It'll be a nice break from the games and stalking. "Jon, we only have two weeks to leave for Arizona, you still want to go, right?" "Of course I do Brooke, I can't wait to leave this place and have some real time with you." "Good, because when we get on that plane, I don't want to talk about this place or anything that has happened here. I need a goddamn break from it all." He kissed the tip of my nose and said he wanted the same thing.

"We have to get Kate a graduation present; should I take Pam with me or do you want to go?" "I'll go, it will be fun," he smiled. We quickly were dressed and headed to the mall. We held hands as we walked the corridors of the mall and I finally felt like he was okay with us being a couple in public. I picked out a journal for Kate. I love mine and this one has an ocean sunset on the cover, it's breathtaking. We left the mall, went back to my room, our room, and just studied. This was normal and I loved it. He spent the night every night for a week. I haven't gone to his fraternity since I walked out before confronting Steph. I didn't miss it one bit. We got a good system down to avoid the housemother too. He took my car to classes and came over after, always horny, so damn insatiable.

He went back to his fraternity and got a ration of shit from the guys telling him he was pussy whipped and he wasn't a true brother anymore. He told them to fuck themselves and shut his door. Nate was in the room and said, "Hey man I almost put out a missing person ad on you. You must really be in hot water with this girl huh." "I don't know what it is about her. She's different from other girls Nate. I need her and she makes me completely insane. I can't function without knowing she's all mine, man. What the fuck? I didn't plan this man, you know who I am. Damn, her kindness and spirit has captured me. Her sense of humor, her devotion to me, it is an addiction to me," Jon said.

"There's nothing wrong with it Jon. She's a

beautiful girl with a heart of gold and if I were you, I'd keep it in your pants to keep her with you," Nate said. "I plan on it; I plan on it. I have to get some sleep man, so I can finish this week of classes and be ready for Arizona. We need this time away; we need to get away from the assholes in this house and psycho Steph! "

"Nate, do you love Noelle," Jon asked. "I think I do. I know that she's a player and I'm trying to balance that. For now, she's been faithful and I like being with her, so yeah, I guess I do love her," Nate said. "We are two peas in a pod aren't we? The funny thing is, Noelle is more my type and Brooke is more your type, how did this happen," Jon questions? "No way could you and Noelle be a couple, you'd wear each other out and need your own infirmary just for the STD treatments," Nate replied. They both laughed and went to sleep.

The next week is going to be crazy, finals and getting ready for Arizona. I can't have any distractions this week. I have to do a mock trial as one of my final grades and I have to kick butt. Jonathon has finals as well and we'll both be studying up until we leave.

Pam and I are busy making flashcards on my room floor. We're making up the songs we do to memorize information, but none of it can be used for the mock trial. I will be the defense attorney for an illegal search and seizure case. I'm excited, but nervous. So much coffee in our systems and not much food, Pam and I found ourselves getting punchy and laughing, we couldn't not study anymore tonight. It was a loss cause.

Pam went to her room and I tried to fall asleep, but my mind was racing and I needed Jonathon to sleep next to me. It was late and I knew he would be sleeping, but I called and they got him. I told him I needed him with me, he said he would be right over. I had to go downstairs and make sure the housemother was asleep and her door closed so he could sneak in. Getting in was always the hard part.

I waited for him at the door and we ran up the stairs like two school kids eating candy. His hair was all in disarray and he looked so cute. I apologized for waking him and he said he couldn't sleep either. No energy for playing around, we just snuggled up and went fast asleep until the alarm clock went off, too early. We grabbed a Kudo for breakfast and both went to class, but we decided that each night we'd have to sleep together.

The butterflies are wreaking havoc in my stomach. I opened the classroom door to what looks like a courtroom. I'm up against the prosecutor who is no one other than Steph. I am going to squash her like a bug. I had to. I presented my case without hesitation and made the points I needed to make. Steph presented her case and her final arguments sucked. She was stumbling over her words and I loved it. The jury came back and found for the defendant, I won. It was an easy win though, but nonetheless I beat that Amazon. Oh Sweet Justice.

She walked out of the courtroom, sulking as the instructors were praising my due diligence and sticking to the facts. It was a great feeling to have this behind me. On my way back to my dorm, I felt like skipping, until Steph came out from behind a tree. She yelled out to me, "you won't win in the end Brooke Fucking Walsh, you wait and see." "Whatever," I said to her and went on my way. Jealousy sure is evil. There's no way her and Jonathon just had a one-night stand, she's obsessed and relentless, or maybe she was just plain crazy.

Jon came by after his classes and dinner and we studied together. We both had a piece of the floor with papers everywhere. I looked over at him with his glasses on and I couldn't concentrate. He was so sexy with his specs on. He felt me looking at him and looked up, smiled. "What are you thinking about my dirty girl," he asked. He closed the book and we made love on top of all the papers, it was a much-needed release with all the stress from finals. "I feel so much better. Thank you sir." "Anytime my dirty girl. I'll never get enough of you. Mmm, your sweet smell and the taste of you, never will I get tired of you." "I'll remember you said that when you're 80 and can't get it up," I chuckled.

At that moment, I thought to myself, I could see me growing old with this guy. The thought of having babies with him excites me. They would be so beautiful and smart like their dad. The simple act of going to bed and waking up next to him every day would be a dream for me. I want that, I want to be with him forever.

He snapped at me and told me to finish the chapter I was on and stop procrastinating. I had to get an A on this final to get a 4.0, and he was right, so back to the books. He cared about my success and that meant so much to me. I finished the chapter and we had to get to sleep quickly, morning was approaching fast. We hopped into bed and I couldn't fall asleep, so he rubbed my hair until I began to sleep.

As I drifted off to sleep, it was so vivid and clear. Never did I want to wake up from this dream. The news came, we were pregnant, and Jonathon was over the moon with excitement. Our first child. I dreamt it was a boy, perfect, chubby little boy with tons of hair. Jonathon was caring and giving while I was pregnant and he was with me every step of the way of delivery. We were a family, and then the dream ended.

I could throw that alarm clock out the window, "stop," it's too early," I yelled. "Get up lazy bones, after today, we're done we're our way to Arizona," saying through his kisses. I smiled and got my ass out of bed.

My final was a breeze and I know I aced it. I hope Jonathon did well on his too. Heading home to pack and clean my room from last night, I stood for a moment and felt warmed by how things were progressing with us. Things have really come together and it's no longer a wonder of his love, it's evident and true.

It's too bad Noelle and I aren't close anymore. She has some good clothes I could have borrowed for our trip. I must bring some sexy things as we're going to be in our own hotel room. I can't wait to board that plane and head the hell out of here.

Meanwhile, Jonathon is at his place packing and he isn't just packing clothes, he said he has some surprises for me when we get there. I can only imagine. Part of me is unsure if I should be scared or excited.

I thought for a second about what Steph said to me yesterday. My stomach got queasy and I had to stop myself from thinking too much. Nothing was going to ruin this trip. Jon snuck in again and came up to my room. He brought with him a ratty old stuffed dog that he had since he was 3 years old. "I know you don't like to fly as I don't, so I thought we could both hold him to make us feel better," Jon said looking like a child. "As long as I'm with you Jonathon, I'll be fine." His final went well. We talked about going to the desert in Arizona, and his imagination ran wild. He has a one tracked mind for sure. We went to sleep and got up early to catch our flight. Thankfully, the airport was only twenty miles away.

We checked our bags and boarded the plane. I, of course was casing the plane for would be terrorists. Fastening our seat belts and listening to the flight attendant's instructions in the event of a crash, my legs went weak and Jon held my hand tight. Once we got up in the air, I was fine and so was he. We had the ratty dog with us too, he would fix everything, Jon says.

We landed and headed to the rental car agency and picked up our car. We were only using it for one day as my sister rented a van for all of us. We drove to the hotel where the family was, we were the last ones to arrive because of finals. Kate was so pretty with her blonde hair and her toned body, I'm so proud of her. She's with her degree in Business Administration. She has plans to open her own sporting goods store; she was the athlete of the family. My brother Rob and my sister Joan were there and my mom and dad, of course.

We ordered in Chinese Food and played cards. Jon fits right in; he makes everyone laugh when he laughs. It was so normal and natural and it was a refreshing change from campus.

Jon and I went to our room to get changed and ready for bed. The graduation was at 9 am and we had to meet for breakfast first, it was going to be an early morning. Jon was unpacking and I saw a bottle of something in his bag and asked him what it was, and he told me, "You'll see." I got into the bed, the sheets were crisp and smelled of bleach, I didn't like the smell, but the pillows were soft and comfortable. Jon got on top of the bed and told me to lie on my stomach. Oh no, he's going to screw me from behind, please, not tonight, I was thinking to myself.

He poured oil on his hands and rubbed them together. He took my t-shirt off and massaged my neck, back and my feet until I fell asleep. I slept through the night and woke up feeling refreshed and ready for the day. All was great.

We ate breakfast with the family and went to the graduation. Kate looked stunning in her cap and gown and she earned her high honors. So proud of my sister, soon, this will be Jon up on the stage receiving his diploma. He's one year ahead of me. After graduation, Jon and I took a walk through some shops and had a nice lunch outside. It was nice to be in warm weather. After lunch, we headed back to the hotel, but Jon spotted a store that he dragged me into. I was so embarrassed; it was a sex toy store. He had no qualms about picking things up and saying, "Wouldn't this be fun," he laughed aloud. I had to leave the store I was horrified in there. He came out with a bag and refused to show me what he purchased. I just knew this was going to be something new for me. I never used any toys before and I wouldn't even know how.

Strolling down the sidewalk to the hotel, we were stunned how beautiful Tucson was. So different from New England, but we both loved New England and the four seasons. The hotel was in front of us and I really needed to take a shower after walking in the heat. When we got in our room, the phone was beeping which meant we had a message. I called the front desk and they gave me the message, it was from Kate. We're meeting in the lobby in an hour and going to dinner, thankfully, this didn't give us enough time to try what Jon had hidden in the bag.

We're going to Mi Nidito (My Little Nest) for dinner, a Mexican restaurant and I was so excited for some real spicy food. I told Jon, "I think I'll wear a dress so I can eat a ton," rubbing my belly. He laughed and it all fit into his plan. It couldn't have been more perfect for him. After I got out of the shower, Jon handed me the bag he brought back from the store and said, "Put them inside of you while we're out, they'll make you crazy and I'll be pleasured by that." I had no idea what they were. "Jon, what are these," I asked. "Ben Wa Balls, you put them inside you, pull on the string and it'll give you sensations. Maybe you'll even cum during dinner, in fact, I'll make sure of it," he said laughing. A bit uncomfortable with this, I succumbed and inserted them. He told me I couldn't wear underwear tonight, he wanted full access.

Walking with the balls inside of me was very strange at first, but I could feel the sensations, "I just hope I don't get seated across from my father at dinner." We both laughed. We all gathered in the lobby and I felt paranoid that everyone knew I had these things in me. We piled in the van that Kate rented and Jon and I went to the very back. It was a bumpy ride back there and Jon was laughing at my expressions. The Ben Wa balls were making their presence known.

We arrived at Mi Nidito and it was a cozy, southwestern atmosphere. I could smell the fiery spices and I couldn't wait to try this real, authentic food. My dad said, "I ordered some special spicy wings for you, I was told nobody can eat them. So, Brooke, are you up for the Challenge?" "Yes dad, bring them on." Hot food was my favorite, the hotter the better for me.

The wings arrived and all eyes were on me, thankfully, dad was at the head of the table and Kate was across from me. I took my first bite of the wing, as I did that, Jon placed his hand under the table, up my dress and tugged on the string of the balls. As I tried to swallow the chicken, my legs started to shake and my eyes watered and I started to choke. It wasn't the spicy wings; it was the orgasm Jonathon just made me have.

Dad laughed at me and said, "I knew you couldn't do it, baby girl. Too hot for even you." I regained my composure and couldn't let my dad down. I took another wing, ate the whole thing, and then begged for a glass of milk. I felt like my mouth was blistering, they were beyond hot wings, but addicting. Much like the balls that were inside of me.

We all ate our meals and laughed and I wanted to give Kate a toast. I had written something up for her. I asked everyone to raise his or her glasses as I had something to say. The entire table said, "We need to leave tonight Brooke, we know how you like to talk."

"Yeah yeah, this is short."

Glasses in hand, I read:

"To Kate, I am so proud of you and proud to call you my sister. You graduated from college with Honors; I can only hope to graduate from college. They all laughed, knowing my high school grades were less than perfect. You will be successful in anything you do and I wish you as much happiness that I have now. Love you sis."

"See, it was short," I snickered. We all tapped our glasses and got ready to leave. Kate got teary-eyed and responded with thanks and gratitude, and especially a thank you to me for not going on for hours, we all laughed. It was a great night with family and Jonathon. This was Jon and I's last night here before returning to reality.

On our way out, Kate called Jon and I over to her and said, "I just want to tell you, whatever you two are doing, keep doing it. You both are glowing and you look so happy." That was very sweet and she was right. Thankfully, she had no idea there were metal balls stuck up my vagina that Jon was pulling on and making me shake under the table. Kate was the best and I really want her to find a guy that will make her as happy as I am.

Kate went on to say, "Brooke you deserve this more than anyone, what you two have is rare. I may have a degree but I don't have love and without it, I'm alone. Treasure each other and Jonathon, I beg you not to break her heart, she is precious." "Kate, I don't intend to break her heart, I only want to please her, love her and be with her forever." We all smiled and piled into the van for our last time.

We all got out of the van and Jon and I gave us

hugs good-bye because we had an early flight back in the morning. Kate and I cried. I'm excited she's planning a trip to stay with me for a weekend at school, so I'll see her soon. Rob, he was his normal dorky self. Joan, she just gave me a quick hug, she's so cold at times. Mom and dad were the best, hugs and dad slipped an envelope to Jon to have him give me. It was a great end to a couple great days.

Jonathon and I walked to the elevator to go to our room. Walking in heels with these balls was no easy task. In the elevator, Jon pulled on the strings and started sucking my lips. With his foot, he pressed the stop button of the elevator. In between floors, the elevator stopped, devouring each other and he put himself in me with the balls in and I screamed, "Holy Shit!" All the way to my throat was tingling and my eyesight became blurry, my legs gave out, and I fell in Jon's arms.

"That's my dirty girl; you liked that, didn't you?" "Oh yeah, it was intense. I thought my heart was going to stop." "I knew you'd like them Brooke," he smiled and held my hand. Back in motion, we got out on our floor and headed to our room. Surprisingly, we hadn't used the Jacuzzi yet so this was necessary before we left.

"Before I forget Brooke, your dad gave me this envelope to give you," Jon remembered. I opened the envelope and there was a crisp hundred-dollar bill and a note that said, "Get something to eat, you're getting too skinny, love dad." If he only knew why I had lost a few pounds, he would kill someone. Jon knew he was giving me money, dad told him I must not be eating because of money. Jon didn't say a word.

"Jonathon," I called from the Jacuzzi, "Join me."

He came in with a white hotel robe on and brought in some candles that he had packed in his bag. He lit the candles and the smell of Lavender filled the room. "How did you know I love lavender?" "I know more about you than you know about yourself, remember?" "Are you going to join me Jon or am I going to be lonely in here with all these bubbles," I seductively asked him. He stepped in and got behind me so I could lean back on him. It was relaxing with the lights off and just the flickers from the candles. The hot bubbles, and the hot body behind me, it felt magical. Jon played with my hair as I leaned back on his chest, giving me small kisses every so often and I fell asleep. He picked me up out of the Jacuzzi and put me to bed.

The morning came, along with the wakeup call. We hurried to get dressed and out the door to the airport. We had to take a cab, which the hotel had arranged for us. The cab driver was Spanish and the only thing we understood him say was, "You in Love?" We smiled and laughed.

The plane ride was uneventful and we slept most of way with the damn stuffed dog between us. We got our luggage and we were going back to our own dorms. I believe in giving space. As much as I want Jon with me all the time, he is in college and has his buddies from his frat. As much as I didn't like many of them, they were his friends and should hang with them. I wouldn't want him to resent me and I trusted him, so it's all good. There was still uneasiness that I felt when he was with his frat brothers because I knew they didn't want him to have a girlfriend. Hell, I think him being single helped the other guys get laid!

I drove up to his fraternity to drop him off and we made out like kids. Once we pried our lips apart, he went inside. I can only imagine the kind of shit he'll get from those assholes. I drove home, reliving our few days in Arizona, I felt so blessed to have such an amazing guy. He made me feel sexy, loved and beautiful. When I'm with him, I'm complete. Exhausted, happy and feeling loved, that's a great combination for a nap. When I got to my room, I put my luggage down, put on a t-shirt and took a long nap.

I slept until 11am today and went to the dining hall with Pam and Jillian. I told them about my trip and the Ben Wa Balls and I think they're going to go buy some for themselves. They were shocked that I even did it, but they said, I have changed, more confident and at ease since I met Jon. I told them, "That's what love is ladies, I am smitten! I never thought I could have sex so much, but with him, I can't get enough." "I had that once, hold onto it tight, it's very rare," said Jillian.

Jon called after lunch and told me there was a special party this weekend for the freshman in the house and no girls were aloud. He went on to say I couldn't stay at his place this weekend. He had to be at the party because he was the President of the fraternity. "Well, that works out great because Noelle told me that a bunch of our friends will be home this weekend and they're all getting together. I'll just go home for the weekend and we'll have our special time when I get back. I'll miss you though. Maybe I'll bring the balls home with me, chuckling." "No, you will not, you are to ever have an orgasm without me, he demanded." "Calm down boy, I was kidding anyway. I don't want an orgasm from anyone but you; you know that and you had better get used to it. I love you Jonathon." "Brooke, I love you too, more than you will ever know."

"Can you come over tomorrow night and sleep," I asked. "Brooke, I 'm sorry. This week isn't great because we're doing some renovations to the house and I have to make sure all is going well." "Well, I guess I'll see you on Sunday when I come back. I'll miss you Kudo. You'll be on my mind the whole time I'm gone." "Brooke, please be good," saying with fear. "Jonathon, trust me for once, please."

Something strange is going on. Jon never gives up an opportunity to be with me and have sex. Maybe it really is just the stress from remodeling the frat house. As much as I trust him, my mind still gets stuck in a place of uncertainty. Thinking about Steph again and why Jonathon called her a cheater. I keep forgetting to ask him. I have to believe in him, the connection we have can't be a lie.

The next few days were spent studying, eating (under my dad's advisement) and catching up on sleep. I'm leaving after class today for home. I'm excited it should be fun to see the high school friends. I'm going to surprise Jonathon with breakfast this morning before he goes to class.

I hurried up, showered, and ran to the dining hall to get him a plate of scrambled eggs; bacon, sausage and English muffins and I slid a Kudo in the box as well. I was racing over to his frat house so I could catch him before class and ran up to his room. The door was ajar, so I walked in. It looked as though Noelle was sleeping in Jon's bed, but I looked over to the other bed and she and Nate were still sleeping. I pulled down the covers from Jon's bed, as I couldn't see the face under the blanket. He was sleeping naked with a blonde girl who was wearing my fucking t-shirt and nothing else. Nobody even woke up when I pulled the covers down. She looks familiar. It dawned on me; she's in my business law class.

I dropped the breakfast on the table and ran out of there. Nobody knew I'd been there. Trembling and nauseas, I had to go to class. I hope that it will help me forget the vision I just saw. I walked in to class and fucking Steph was there. I was in no mood for her this morning. "How is your morning Sunshine," Steph asked sarcastically. I replied, "Go to hell." "What's the matter, your love life falling apart," she said smiling. I had to walk away before I lost it.

How does she know everything? I hate her and pretty much hate everyone right now. I walked out of class to go puke and just went and got my things and drove home. When I got home, the house was empty and I was happy about it. I didn't want to talk to anyone except for my cat. I went to my room and the cat was sleeping on my bed as she always was. I lay myself next to her and sobbed until I had no more tears.

So much for renovations, the only thing Jon was renovating was someone's cunt. How could he do this to me? I wish I could cheat on him, but that's Noelle's style, not mine. Oh, great, I'll see her tonight. She was sleeping like a baby right next to my boyfriend banging some blonde slut from my class. She never cared to let me know. She's an evil bitch.

This isn't going to ruin my weekend with my

friends. I need this after the display I witnessed this morning. He can wonder and worry about what I'm doing; I'm just fine with that. I'm going out and having a good time no matter what.

Mom came home as I was leaving to go to meet the gang, she gave me a peck on the cheek and off I went. I was heading to Holly's house, which was across town, and we were all going to hang there. The whole crew was there, even Josh. He looked good and after a few beers and my visual, he was looking better. We talked and he asked how I was and I lied, of course and told him great. Noelle was watching us like hawks and I was making sure I gave her no indication of anything; I had no trust left for her. She had the audacity to come up to me and ask, "why didn't you say good-bye to Jon before you left to come home, he was upset you know." "Was he upset before or after the blonde got out of his bed this morning," I asked.

She claimed she had no idea I was there this morning. "Noelle, let me tell you something, if I saw your boyfriend with another girl, I would stop it from happening because that's what friends do. You are so self- centered, you only think about yourself and you say nothing, that isn't a friend," I rambled on. "Brooke, I was asleep when he came in, I swear, I didn't wake up until it was too late." "So, you were awoken by their fucking noises?" "Don't make me answer that Brooke." "Please, just get the hell away from me Noelle."

I went downstairs and did some shots and played cards with a few of the guys. I had no idea what I was doing, but I won a few pots. The room began to spin as I had way too much to drink and I needed to go home, but I couldn't drive. Josh volunteered to give me a ride home; he said he was leaving anyway. Part of me thought about it for a second, but I never could. My answer was NO! Sandy gave me a ride home and I had to sleep with one leg on the floor to stop the spinning. I didn't get much sleep because I was puking all night. I woke up with a cement block on my head and begged mom to make me some soup.

"Rough night," mom asked, as I crawled down the stairs. I told her, "Lower your voice and yes, it was a rough night." Jon called for you this morning again, you should call him back," mom said. "No, I can't talk to him right now. I'm going to throw up again." I had to run back to the bathroom. Mom made me the soup and made me eat some, after three bowls, I started feeling human again. I went upstairs and took a much-needed shower to get all the puke out of my hair. After my shower, I sat on my bed and grabbed my journal out of my bag. Hearing my mom telling me to write how I'm feeling when she gave it to me for Christmas.

March 2

I feel like shit. I drank too much last night but I needed to. Josh was at the party and I felt nothing for him, a friend, yes, but nothing else. I think he thought he could get laid anytime he came home when I was around, but he's sadly mistaken. It did feel good though to let him know he no longer had a hold over me.

Who is Jonathon? Has this whole relationship been a lie? He said he had changed, he said he loved me; he wanted me to be his. How could he do this to me, to us? My heart is broken and right now, I hate him. I don't think I can ever forgive him for this. He broke my heart.... the end for today.

I lay in bed for the rest of the day and watched TV with the cat. Mom called up to me and told me Jon was on the phone. He must have a guilty conscience. I got up, went, and took the call in my mom's room. "Hello." "Hey babe, why haven't you called me back?" "I've been busy and today I'm sick Jonathon." "What's the matter, are you okay?" "Yes, just hung-over." He wasn't happy that I got drunk without him and he couldn't monitor my every move, but I didn't care. "Jon, I can't talk, I feel like crap and I'll see you tomorrow, I have to give you something." "Okay, well hurry back, I miss you, and love you." I didn't respond with anything more than an OK and we hung up.

Hearing him tell me he loves me makes me want to puke again. Does he think I'm that stupid? Well, I'm not and he's going to learn that quickly. How can he act as if nothing happened? He was in bed with a girl and she was wearing my clothes.

I crawled back into bed and slept into the morning. I got up and went down to the kitchen, had a bite to eat with mom and headed back to school. I had to prepare for what I was going to say when I went to see Jon and give him this; but I'm not rushing over there. He'll expect me to and I'm not. I'll go tonight, today, I'm going shopping with Pam. Shopping cures everything at least temporarily.

While shopping with Pam, I bought a pair of Liz Claiborne linen pants and a white button down shirt. I had to look great when I saw Jonathon tonight. I want to make him feel as guilty as possible and to realize what he just gave up. After hours of shopping, we went back and had dinner at the dining hall. Then Pam came to my room and got me all prettied up to see Jon. She had no idea what happened, but she knew I wanted to look extra special for him. She was my personal beautician. It was nearing 9:00 and I had to head over as he had called 4 times since I got home and I never called him back.

I pulled into the side parking lot to park and opened the side door, which I never use, but it was dark and it was the closest door. As I opened the door, Jon was walking out. He was drinking and it was obvious. He was looking right through me, he raised his voice to me, "Oh there you are you whore." He took his hands and ripped the crotch out of my brand new pants. "What are you doing Jonathon," I screamed. "You fucked him! I can't believe you fucked him!" he yelled in my ear.

"Who did I fuck this time Jon," I yelled back. "Mr. Baseball!" "Who is Mr. Baseball?" "You know that Josh you fucked for years? You were so in love with him, remember," he screamed. Coming closer to me, he ripped my shirt open and shouted, "Is this what he did to you?" "Leave me alone!" I screamed and ran to my car. He was running after me. I started my car, put it in reverse, he opened the door and I fell out. The car ran over my legs and my stomach. I was lying there, not able to move right away and the car was now in the middle of the parking lot with the motor still running.

In the parking lot next door, a guy witnessed the whole thing. He came out from nowhere and beat the shit out of Jonathon. I managed to crawl to a friend's next door and they brought me to the hospital. They rushed me right in as I looked like I had been raped with a ripped out crotch and a button less shirt. They asked me what happened and I told them it wasn't Jon's fault. I tried to explain to them he just opened the door to stop me and I fell out. After he pulled me out of the car, I don't think he realized it was in motion because he was drunk. I didn't want to press charges. It was an accident and someone had already beaten him up bad.

I had a broken rib, multiple bruises and yet another sprain neck. My knee split open and I had six stitches put in. I left the hospital with another neck brace, a brace around my ribs and crutches. As much pain as I was in, I was concerned for Jonathon, he looked like he was badly beaten. I begged my friend Dawn to drop me off at Jon's fraternity. I had to see if he was okay. Dawn didn't want me to go there, but I insisted and my car was there, not that I could drive. It was about 3am at this time and his fraternity house was rocking.

I hobbled in and went to his room, surprisingly, his door was open and the lights were on. I walked in by my crutches and saw him sitting there…alone. Still drinking. His left eye was swollen shut, his lips were huge and crusted over with blood, the right side of his face was black, and blue. He looked like a monster.

"Are you alright," he asked. "I'm okay. I'm pretty sore. My rib is broken." "Brooke, you have to believe me, I didn't know you had the car in reverse. I'm sorry! I didn't mean for that to happen, really, I am so sorry," he cried. He was filthy drunk and I didn't want this to get ugly again, so I put him in bed and I slept on the couch. I still loved him and I wanted to make sure he was okay.

I heard him groaning all night in pain and a part of me was happy about it. He wasn't the only one hurt. I was hurt too and all for what? Some figment of his imagination that I slept with Josh, he was wrong again and I'm paying for it. Ringing in my ear, I hear my brother Rob's voice, "I trust him, and he's a good guy." Hearing the words of my brother reminded me that I had to give Jonathon something. I thought I would have this forever and treasure it.

The morning came and I could barely move. I was so sore and my ribs were killing me. He was sore and couldn't open his left eye at all and his mouth was swollen. He told me to come and lay with him, but I refused. I reminded him that I came over last night to give him something. "Oh, I hope it's an icepack," he said. "No, Jon, it's not, sorry," I said. I took the pearl ring off my finger, opened his hand, and gave it to him. "What are you doing? I didn't know the car was on and I said I was sorry Brooke! Didn't you hear me," he said in a panic.

"Jonathon, this has nothing to do with last night," I said. "Then why are you giving this back to me," he yelled. "Friday when you woke up, did you have breakfast on your desk," I asked. "Yes, it was cold and the eggs were green when I woke up. I think Nate brought it for me because he knew I would need something because I was so messed up the night before." "Does Nate bring you Kudos too," I asked. "What are you talking about Brooke? There was no Kudo," he said.

"No, Jonathon, Nate didn't bring you breakfast, I did." "Oh, then why didn't you wake me up before you left," he asked. "Are you fucking kidding Jonathon? My voice is getting louder. You are a sick bastard; do you know that?"

"Why," he asked sounding very confused. He had no idea what I was talking about, "What did I do

Brooke? Please tell me," he begged. "I saw you Jonathon. I saw you naked in bed with that girl and she was wearing my fucking t-shirt and nothing else," I said crying.

"Brooke, what are you talking about? There was nobody here with me. I went to bed alone and woke up alone," he pleaded. "Good try Jon! Too bad I saw it with my own eyes and Noelle even told me that your fucking noises woke her up," I explained. "She is lying! I was with nobody," he screamed. "Then you're calling me a liar too because I saw you in bed with her," I said through my tears. "Brooke, I swear to you, I don't know what you think you saw but I was with nobody," he insisted.

"I'm done Jonathon. I can't do this anymore. We are over," I cried. "Brooke, no! Don't do this! I swear I didn't do anything and I don't care if you fucked Mr. Baseball, I forgive you," he screamed out. "I didn't fuck Josh; I don't know why you would think that. I'm not like you! I'm committed to you and I believed in our love and trust," I cried harder. He screamed at me, "Noelle told me you went home with him." "She's a lying bitch! I did not," I yelled. "Sandy brought me home and I left my car at Holly's because I had a lot to drink because of you."

"I'm glad you got your face punched in because nobody is going to want to screw you looking like that. Just maybe you'll have to be celibate for a while; if you can handle it. We're both bruised up because of your insecurity and mistrust, when the one you shouldn't trust is yourself. Good-bye Jon! Oh, just one more thing, I really loved you and I thought you loved me too. I'm the fool once again," I said with a shaky voice.

Walking as fast I can with all the apparatuses I had to use, I passed Noelle in the hallway. "Noelle, you best stay the hell out of my life. You are sick and twisted just like Steph, lying to make me look bad, you are pathetic," I snapped. I tripped her with my crutch and laughed in her face then walked out. I got in my car and carefully drove myself to the park. I needed to be alone and think. Torturing myself, I went and sat under the Weeping Willow Tree where Jon and I had one of the most memorable nights. It wasn't torture after all. It was good to sit and reflect on how strong our connection was, and I had to find clarity in all of this. My mind was wandering back to him and me under this same Willow Tree, making love. It dawned on me, he had low self-esteem too and sex was what he was good at and made him feel powerful and confident. Always needing reassurance that I was his and controlling me, it was all part of his insecurities within himself. I suddenly felt sympathy for him. I could relate. I always gave and did things for people to be accepted. He gave his body and by pleasuring girls, it raised his confidence. He felt in control. It made me wonder what shattered his self-esteem; he had everything going for him.

Thoughts moved to Noelle and Steph, were they in this together, I wondered. I know they've hung out together, maybe they're in cahoots. But why? Noelle was beautiful, she could have any guy she wanted and Steph, she's just in a dreamland. So many things are racing through my mind. The one constant thought remains, despite it all, I love this guy and it scares me we are over. My heart is empty, I have a pit in my stomach and my body is aching all over. I love him. I can't imagine myself not with him. How do I go on? I need a distraction.

I have to get back and finish my project for my morning class, maybe that'll help get my mind off this. Trying to pull myself up off the ground, my ribs are burning with pain and I want to die for more than one reason. I got myself up after a few minutes and drove to my dorm. I showered and got into my sweats and went to put his Navy t-shirt on and decided to put another one on instead. It's just too hard right now to have him near me.

Pulling out my papers for my project, I'm interrupted by a knock at my door. I said to come in and in walked Noelle.

"Get out of my room," I said to her. "Brooke, there's something you need to know," Noelle stated. "Unless someone is dying, I don't care what you have to say," I said. "No, Brooke, you have to listen to me, please, it's for your own good," she begged. "What could you possibly have to say that would be for my good," I asked. "When you came to Jon's room on Friday, before you went home, I knew that you were coming. I overheard you say it to Pam. I'm not proud of this. You know how awful I am in Accounting it's the only non-coloring class I have. I am failing the class and I was desperate. I made a deal with Steph that I would try and break you and Jon up and she would do my accounting work for me," Noelle said.

"You what? How may I ask have you been trying to do this," I yelled. Noelle began to blurt it all out, "Jon was really drunk Thursday night and he passed out. That was a perfect opportunity for me to get Steph's friend from your Business Law Class to get in bed with him. I knew he wasn't going to wake up and I knew there was no way he could get it up, so I thought it was okay. Melissa is her name, she agreed to do it because she knew how much Steph liked Jon and I need to pass Accounting," she said.

"So, you're telling me that you staged this whole thing and Jon had no role in it," I asked. "Yes, he had no idea and still doesn't. It gets worse. I wasn't sure if he did know, so I had to tell him you slept with Josh because I knew that would cause a lot of problems with you two," Noelle said guiltily.

"Noelle, you're insane! This is all for a passing grade? You would hurt someone like this that was your friend? You know how much I love him; you know I would never cheat on him. What you've done will never be forgiven," I told her. "Brooke, you've always been well liked and you didn't have to sleep your way there. Everyone thinks you're so fucking sweet and cute. The only thing guys like about me is my body and sex. I don't have your personality. No guy has ever loved me for just me. I know Jon loves you and I wanted you to suffer as I do. Everyone adores you, you're funny, pretty, caring and all I have are my looks and my body," Noelle rambled on.

"Nate loves you Noelle. If you could open your eyes and think of something other than your clothes and money, you would see that and have that happiness. Noelle, you're too afraid to settle down because you may be missing someone better. You fuck your way through all the guys to see if they're the one and it's repulsive. If you love yourself Noelle, maybe someone can fully love you. Spreading your legs for everyone doesn't display love and respect for yourself. How do you expect anyone to fully love you," I asked?

"I have slept with over 70 guys Brooke, it's too late for me, "she said. "Noelle, it's never too late to change and I suggest if you want true happiness and love in your life, you do just that. I actually hope you do find your happiness Noelle. I'm not like you who wants to ruin people's happiness." "Maybe I'll try to be more like you," Noelle replied. "No, you need to be you! The real you; not some cover-up girl. If you have insecurities face them, if you want to change, you have to stop what you have always thought and did, otherwise, nothing will change."

"I have to study now Noelle. I'm really not sure if I should thank you or punch you, but for now I'll do neither." She walked out the door. Is there ever a dull moment, I asked myself? Jon didn't screw that girl and he really didn't know she was there. Then the lovely Noelle told him I slept with Josh. I was run over by my own car, he got beat up by some on looking stranger all because Noelle wants to pass her class and Steph wants to get back into Jon's pants. This is fucked up! After finally finishing my project, I crawled into bed and thought about what to do. I'm overwhelmed and I'm not sure I can handle the drama for a while.

Jon and I met for coffee on neutral territory. His face was healing since a week ago when I last saw him. He had to have his contact removed surgically, as it was stuck in the back of his eye. My neck was feeling better along with my knee but my ribs still hurt. We sat and talked and I found myself a bit uneasy and quiet. "Have you spoken to Noelle," I asked to break the ice. "She came over and explained everything and I did everything not to hit her. Nate held me back. She and Nate broke up. He was disgusted that she would do that and realized she was all about herself," Jon said. "I can't say that he's wrong, but I'm sad they broke up because I think she was the closest to happiness she's ever been," I said. "How can you still wish her good Brooke, after what she did to us," he asked. "Jonathon, everyone deserves to be happy and loved even when they do bad things. I won't ever forget what she has done, don't get me wrong, but I wish her happiness. Wishing people bad isn't healthy, it's a waste of good energy," I told him.

"Are we okay," Jon asked. After a long bit of silence, I said, "I still love you Jonathon, but I need some time to process this all and I think you need some time to figure out if I'm who you want." "Brooke, you're the only one I want," he said. "Jonathon, you have physically hurt me twice and it was all because you didn't trust me or my love. If I'm who you really want then time away will make it better," I said and I got up to leave. "Wait Brooke, can I kiss you," he nervously asked. "Yes, you may," so he put his lips on mine as softly as possible and my heart began to race. He was holding my hand and I had to break away from his hold and leave.

I stooped down behind the coffee shop and cried. I miss him so much and I love him so much but I have to be away from him for a while. It hurts it really hurts. I keep telling myself we'll be stronger for it. At least that's what my mom always told me. I have to trust my gut even though it hurts right now. Knowing he had nothing to do with the girl in his bed and no knowledge of it, the fact still remains that he has hurt me physically.

The days go on, I see Steph at class, and she is happier than I've ever seen her. She's kissing my ass and trying to talk to me because she thinks Jon and I are over. Little does she know, we still love each other and we're just taking a break but I'll play her game. Bring it on Amazon.

"Brooke, do you have your white T-Shirt," Pam yelled to me. "Yeah, are we leaving now," I yelled back. "In a few minutes," she said. Tonight we're all going to a new fraternity and they're having a graffiti party. We have to wear plain white t-shirts so everyone can write on them. This is my first fraternity party that I have been to since I met Jon; he didn't let me go to them. I somewhat feel like I am betraying him, but we're not together right now, so that's my own issue. We've talked and met for coffee and lunch but there's been nothing physical in over a month. Which really sucks, but it has to be this way for a little longer.

I have a bad cold and I don't plan to stay out late, but I have to go and try to have fun. This fraternity is clean and beautiful inside and the guys are respectful to girls, unlike Jon's fraternity. I stayed by Pam's side and watched guys writing all over her shirt and I wasn't comfortable with anyone writing on mine, so I said no. Pam didn't pressure me to let them, she knew how I was and I wasn't feeling well.

After a couple of hours of drinking ginger ale, I started coughing and spit up blood. I was scared and walked to Jon's fraternity, I don't know what possessed me, but I needed him now. Maybe enough time has passed. I walked into his fraternity and ran up the stairs to his room, his door was wide open and the lights were all on. I lay down on the couch under my yellow comforter that I had given him when he got the new room.

I started to fall asleep and I heard his voice coming down the hall, but his wasn't the only one I heard. I stayed under the covers, including my head. He walked in and I heard him say, "Do you need to go to the bathroom first?" She said, "No". I heard the waves from the waterbed and my heart was about to come out of my chest, I stayed under the covers for a minute longer until I heard the snap of her bra.

I couldn't contain myself anymore, I jumped out from under the covers and turned to them, her tits were staring right at me and thankfully, he was still clothed. The funny thing was the girl was on Nate's bed. He would have screwed her in his bed. She was a chubby girl, with black curly hair and not pretty at all. She wasn't hog material, but she wasn't in his league either.

Jon was drunk, again, and he was speechless when he saw me. The girl had no idea who I was. I took the long flimsy mirror off the wall that I had given him and smashed it over his head. I ran out of the room where his best friend was just outside the door. He grabbed me and I was hysterical, he was hugging me and yelling for Jon to come out of the room. When Jon came out of the room and saw Nate hugging me, he punched him in the face. He lost it, "You don't touch my girl!" The tit girl walked out and left. I tried to stop Jon from punching Nate, but I couldn't. How dare he think I'm his girl and be in his room about to fuck another girl?

The guys calmed down a bit and the three of us went back into the room. Sick as a dog and add this to it, I feel like I'm going to die. "Brooke, I didn't know you were coming here. I thought we were broken up for a while." "Apparently you didn't know I was coming over. I would hope you wouldn't bring a slut to your room knowing I was going to be here! You asshole!"

"What made you come here," he asked. "I'm sick and I started coughing up blood and I needed you," I told him. Knocking his beer back, he slurred, "I'm sorry. are you okay now?" "No Jon, I'm worse, thanks to you," I said while slapping him across the face. Nate tried to calm us both down and said that there had been too much beer involved tonight and we have all done things we didn't mean to do tonight. "In Jon's defense, you were broken up Brooke," Nate said. "I know, but I didn't think he would screw the first thing that came along." "I didn't screw her," he started stumbling toward me. "You would have if I didn't pop up from the covers. Nate, he fucking punched you in the face for hugging me for Christ Sakes, how is that okay," I yelled again.

"I keep screwing up Brooke. I love you and I need you back. I promise I'll change, please," he was begging. "You're right about one thing, you keep screwing up. Jon, my heart can't take all of this uncertainty, we need to get out of here and figure this all out. Right now, you're too drunk to have a rational conversation and I feel like crap. I'm going to sleep on the couch so I can make sure you do not wander to another girl." "Can't you sleep with me, Brooke," he pouted. "No Way! You don't deserve it."

The next morning, Jon woke up, went, and took a shower while I was still sleeping. He got dressed, woke me up, and said, "You need to get up, we're going somewhere." He drove me home in my car to take a shower and to get some clothes. He wouldn't tell me where we were going, just to pack a bag.

We got on the highway and drove for an hour. He pulled down a dirt road and drove to the end, where there was a small cabin on a lake. It was made of logs and surrounded by trees on the side and beach sand in the front. A beautiful April morning, the birds were out singing and the sound of the lake churning from a passerby boat was all very calming. This was his friend Rick's place from home and he was letting us stay here for a few days if we wanted. Jonathon was looking for the hide a key to take me inside, once he found it, we walked in. It was breathtaking, the main room was wood, with a bear carpet and a there was a deer head hanging over the stone fireplace. There were two couches and two rocking chairs in the room and a bar situated in the back of the room with three high top bar stools. There was floor to ceiling windows on each side of the fireplace that looked straight out to the lake.

"Do you like it Brooke?" "Very much Jonathon, but what are we doing here?" "You told me you wanted to get out of the campus, so I called Rick and asked him if we could come here. We can stay for a few days if you want." "I have classes Jonathon and you have graduation in a couple weeks, how can we skip like this?" "I'm not concerned about school. My only concern is you and having you mine again. I can no longer be away from you Brooke."

I sat down on the couch and he came to sit next to

me. I was trembling as he grabbed my hand. "Why are you trembling?" "Jon, I'm scared of you and I'm scared to fall into your trap again." He leaned over and kissed me so I couldn't talk anymore. Tears fell on his nose and I realized that I needed him more than ever. "Please don't be scared of me Brooke, I love you." I reached under his shirt to feel his chest and he lifted my shirt over my head. He didn't touch me right away; he just stared down at me. Bringing my pants down to my ankles, he continued to stare. "I have missed you so much Brooke." "Your body is beautiful and I want it all to myself, now." As much as I wanted to stop him, I couldn't. He was the love of my life, despite it all; I wanted and needed him too.

Kissing me and sucking my neck to leave yet another mark, my body was quivering and I fell weak to his touch. His tongue is circling around my breasts while his hands are touching between my legs. "You are so wet; I knew you wanted me too. I'm going to make you come like never before babe."

Throbbing and swelling, he put his mouth on me; he opened my lips and put his tongue inside, sucking all of my juices. My pants are still wrapped around my ankles, so I can't maneuver myself away.

My thighs went dead, and the sensations ran all the way up to my head, I couldn't take it anymore. He kept licking and massaging my clit until I exploded without control. He smiled at me, proud and I pulled him inside of me. It was a feeling I missed so much. The passion and the feeling of him filling me up quickly was what I needed from him. He came so quick, which made me believe he hadn't had sex in a while, since we last had over a month ago.

"Brooke, I want to make love to you all day over

and over again. I want to make you feel loved and wanted, because you are. I want you to be one with me." "All day, with breaks in between I hope," I said smiling. We laughed and got up and walked down by the lake. We were all alone; nobody was around because it wasn't yet the season. He brought out a blanket and rolled it out on the sand. For this instance, everything is erased. It was him and I, love, forgiveness and trust. He pulled my ring out of his pocket and placed it back on my finger and kissed it, "You will wear this and be mine." I was his, even when we were split up but I wanted him to be mine back.

I asked him, "How do I know you're mine?" He answered by pinning a pin on my shirt and I looked down to see it and it was his fraternity pin, this meant we were pre-engaged. I only know of one other person who was pinned and they did get married, so I was ecstatic and I knew he was now all mine. I was so excited; I got up and ran into the lake taking my clothes off as I was running. I felt that by jumping in the cold water, it would clean all the negativity away. It was now in the past. He followed behind me and held me in the cold lake water. I kissed his mouth, he opened it with his teeth, and I wrapped my legs around him, naked in the cold lake water.

We got out of the water, went back to the blanket, and made love once again. This was our private beach for the time being. It was truly amazing. He made me feel exceptional. We were freezing from being wet so we got up, went inside, and made some lunch. Lucky for us, there was food in the freezer. We found chicken fingers and French fries and cooked them up in the oven. They had hot sauce in the fridge and that was all

I needed. We flicked the switch to start the gas fireplace and we sat, ate, and watched the fire. He began teasing me about how I loved sex as much as he did. I replied, "It's you that makes me like this, I love sex with you and I'm going to be a very dirty girl later." "Brooke, I can't wait! I love when you're a dirty girl! Even when you're a dirty you're still so pure to me though." "I don't want to be pure tonight," I rasped.

After lunch, we took a long nap and when we awoke, it was getting dark out. I got up with just a t-shirt on and stood in front of the window looking out at the lake. The calmness of the lake and watching the ducks swim by brought me to complete clarity. I had been searching for clarity since going back to the Weeping Willow tree and I have just found it. I heard him stir and wake up and he whispered, "You look beautiful, don't move."

He came behind me and kissed my neck, wrapped his arms around me and stood with me watching the ducks swim by. "What are you thinking about, young lady?" "I'm thinking I know it's a risk being with you Jon and loving you but I want to take that risk. I love you and I know that when we leave the campus, we'll be together forever. There may be more bumps in the road, but when we're out of that environment, we'll be one." He smiled and agreed.

I kissed him and he put his hand between my legs, I then pushed him down on the bear rug. I began stroking his shaft and licking the top of his head, with my hand, I cupped his balls, moved my mouth to them, and took them in my mouth, he was moaning for me not to stop. I placed my head in between his legs. I stroked him some more and put my finger in his ass and started bobbing down on him, taking his cock and rubbing it against the roof of my mouth. Then back to small licks of his head, he's going to come, but I'm not ready, I want him inside of me, hard and fast.

I grabbed his hand, pulled him up and over to the bar stools that were staring at me. I pushed him down on the stool and crawled on top of him, he is deep in me and I'm rocking back and forth, looking into his eyes, he pulled me tight to him and filled me up. "Oh, my dirty girl," he pants, "I love you."

"Did you like that," I asked laughing. "More than you know." The night continued with us laughing and toying with each other. Then I told him that I had made a big decision. He looked scared and asked, "What decision?" "I'm transferring to a new school for my final year back at home." After he graduated, I didn't want the reminders of the pain that I had felt and needed to focus on school.

He was shocked at first, happy but then he thought about being in the same town as Josh and it made his mind spin. "What makes you want to do that," he asked. "Jonathon, with you not there, I don't want the constant reminders of the bad that happened. I want to start anew with you, in new environments as far away from that campus as we can." "Brooke, Josh is in your hometown that concerns me." I reassured him that there was nothing to worry about and I would always be his, no matter where I lived. We talked about where he was going to live after graduation and it was dependent upon where he got a job or not, so it was up in the air. His graduation was in two weeks and things were surely going to change with us living in different states, but we committed to make it work.

Taking one last look around this log cabin and

seeing that we did not miss a spot to have sex on, it made me smile. Very sore in the lower region, we slowly walked to the car to head back to hell campus. It was a great retreat for us and I feel confident in us again. Jon took my hand, kissed it, and said, "My dirty girl, oh how you have a hold over me." "Right back at you, Kudos." What a crazy ride this has been, things are great, things are awful, but at the end of the day, Jon has me under his spell, no matter what. I'm glad he thinks of me as pure, but I like to be not so pure when I'm with him, the dirtier the better sometimes, not always, but sometimes. We had a nice ride back; each of us caught each other staring at one another and laughed. We were madly in love even with all of the issues we have come across.

"Brooke, you're the best I have ever had. It doesn't matter how many times we've had sex together. You still, each and every time make me wild." "Well, Jonathon Sears, I think you know you're the best I have ever had. You're the only person that has ever given me an orgasm." "Yes, and I will never forget the look on your face that first night. You really didn't know what was happening, did you?" "Not a clue, you're my true first in every way that matters Jonathon." "And you are my first as well Brooke and I love you so much." We sat back and reflected for the rest of the ride home.

The final week of school is here. I couldn't be happier to be nearing my escape from this place, no more bullshit, no more frat parties, no more Steph.

One more week and then it's sayonara! Walking to the dining hall with Pam, wearing Jon's jacket and the shiny new pin on the collar, I'm standing proud as we approach Steph walking out of the dining hall in front of us.

I couldn't hold back, "nice try Steph, you made us even closer you fucking bitch," I yelled to her. She came up to me, got right in my face, and said, "This isn't over, I told you before, I will win in the end"! "You have nothing he wants Steph, so spare yourself the humiliation and besides, he's moving away from here and you'll never see him," I gleamed at her. "I have so much more than you can give him," she snarled. I turned and laughed to Pam and told Steph to keep on dreaming and walked away.

Pam finally saw the obsession in this girl's eyes about Jon, it gave her chills that this girl wasn't giving up, and something bad was about to happen to me. "What's that look on your face Pam?" "That Steph is dangerous, Brooke, and I'm afraid something bad will happen to you," Pam stated. "Don't be silly," I said, "we'll all be leaving this place in a week, Jon is graduating and she'll be out of our lives." "I surely hope so for your sake," Pam said. "Everything will be just fine when we leave this place Pam, I can't wait." She looked at me and said, "I hope you know what you're doing." "I'm doing what everyone should do; I'm following my heart Pam."

We went inside and ate and Noelle asked if she could join us, reluctantly, we agreed. She was trying and I felt sorry for her after what she shared with me. "So, Noelle, are you and Nate back together," I asked. "Yes, we are and he's coming to stay in Rhode Island with me for the summer," she said. "I'm happy for you

Noelle, I really am," I said and she smiled.

We got up after eating and we all headed to class, thankfully, Steph didn't show up. I have had enough of her for the rest of the time here. In walked Melissa, the girl that was essentially hired to get in bed with Jon and I stared at her, she was beautiful, at that moment I wanted to run out of the class, but I didn't. She looked over to me, shined her pearly whites at me, and mouthed, "I am sorry!"

After class, I ran home and called Kate. She was coming down for Jon's graduation; she was never able to come before because of all the drama and I couldn't tell her about it. She was going to help me pack my things and she was renting another van to help get all my things back home. She was coming down on Thursday and graduation was Friday. I'm going to try my best to keep her away from Noelle, who knows what things she would tell Kate.

I'm so excited to see her! In between the rest of my classes, I was packing my things and I found an old Kudo. It was smashed under my bed, it reminded me of when Jon set up my room and I was now yearning for him. I threw my boxes down and drove over to see him. He was writing his speech for graduation when I walked in. He was looking down with his glasses on and typing and didn't notice me walk in, so I went behind him and whispered in his ear, "I want to fuck you!"

He swiveled his chair around and brought me to him. "No, I want you to fuck me, now, hard," I repeated. He got hard right away and he put me up against the wall and pounded into me like a machine. It was rough and painful, but I needed it and I wanted it that way. "What has gotten into you, my dirty girl?

"It's going to be a few days that we'll be alone; so I wanted to make sure I could still feel you Jon. "
"That's what I like to hear," he said and bit the tip of my nose.

"Got to go, thanks for that," I started walking out laughing. He just stared at me and laughed. "See you tomorrow night for dinner with Kate and your parents. Be good and think of me. I'll have my balls in at dinner," then I winked at him. That just blew him away and thanks to Steph; she made me gain the courage to show him I'm all he needs, another nail in her coffin.

Rushing back to my dorm to get things packed, I can smell him on me, between my legs is sticky from him and I'm raw, but feeling great about myself. Steph will never win, make no mistake, I'll do whatever I have to do to keep my man. If its sex he needs, I will give it, if it's love, I will give it, he's mine and will stay mine.

Feeling overly energetic and confident, I filled box after box and stacked them all up by the door to be ready to load up in the van. I had my desk to clean out and I am pretty much done. So many notebooks, but one stood out to me, and it wasn't mine, it was Noelle's, Jon must have grabbed it by mistake when moving my things to this room.

Curiosity was killing me, so I sat on the edge of my bed and started flipping through the pages, thinking I was going to see her coloring, wondering if she had talent other than spreading her legs. I turned the page and saw Jon's name on it.

It read:

Jonathon is so hot. I never thought he would really like Brooke; I thought he would fuck her and throw her out like he did to all the others. Why did I ever set them up? Of course, she ends up loved. I hate her. I am so much prettier than she is and he rejected me, what is wrong with me?

Flipping through the pages some more, I came upon this writing:

Hey Steph, tonight is the night, we are finally going to make Brooke hurt as much as we do. She will freak out when she walks in the morning and finds him in bed with Melissa; make sure you tell her not to start laughing. This is the ticket for you. You promise you will do my Accounting, because if you are not going to follow through, I will just fuck him myself and you will get nothing.

Noelle, I am in 100%. Everything is in place and Melissa is heading over at 5am, make sure the door is unlocked. And leave her t-shirt out for her to put on that was a good idea.

Oh, and by the way, don't you dare fuck him!

I won't, you are brilliant, what a perfect plan, she will be crushed and never forgive him.

See you tomorrow after the performance and I will bring you the homework you need to pass in. The library is a great place for us to conspire, don't you think? I cannot wait to see her in class tomorrow, all weepy and sad.

Meet you at 10 am in front of the double doors Steph, where we can exchange goods.

Those fucking bitches; they had it all masterminded. Sick and twisted. I know what Steph was giving Noelle, but what was Noelle giving Steph in front of the double doors? I can't wait to get the fuck out of here and away from this crap.

I threw the notebook in a box and headed out to pick up my dress for dinner tomorrow night. I'm so excited to try it on after the tailor took it in for me. With white spaghetti straps, white over the breasts and lavender on the bottom, it's simple, but stunning. Its 2 inches below my knee so heels are necessary. I tried it on and it fit perfectly. Swirling in front of the mirror, I find myself thinking about the Ben Wa Balls and Jon's hand going up my dress; it has gotten very hot in here. I changed back into my jeans, took the dress, and hung it in my car. One more stop, the jewelers to pick up Jon's graduation gift.

A gold band with lines on it and a beautiful face with the date on it too. I hope he loves this watch; I can't wait to see the inscription I had them engrave in it. The door buzzed as I walked into the beautiful showroom of jewelry and Fred pranced out from the back and room and said, "Miss Walsh, I have your beautiful gift right here and I made sure it was perfect for you."

He handed me the watch, it was beautiful, and I turned it to make sure they engraved it with the right words. Kudos, I am yours, Brooke. "This is perfect Fred, thank you so much. Would it be possible for you to put it in a larger box than that one, he likes to play games like that," I asked? "Of course Miss Walsh, I like those games too," he chuckled. He handed me the bag and off I went.

Kate was beeping the horn as she pulled in, I ran out to get her and we hugged tight, she represented so much to me. It was great to have her here. I was happy she didn't come during the school year as she may have heard things while she was here; I didn't want her to know what had been happening all year long. She would worry about me and she wouldn't understand.

We went up to my room and started bringing boxes down, we passed Pam in the hall, I introduced her to Kate, and she lugged the boxes with us. We laughed a lot while loading the van; it was awesome to have Kate here.

The two of us went back to my room to break and to catch up on life. Kate saw the picture of Jon and me and said, "You're so lucky Brooke, he seems perfect." "Nobody is perfect Kate, but I do love him even with his many imperfections." She then asked me how the sex was and I blushed and went on to tell her, words really can't describe it, this may be where his perfection comes in and we laughed. "How about you Kate, any love in your life," I asked.

"Funny you should ask Brooke, I met Justin a couple months ago and we have been together almost every day since, this is the first time being away from him." "Where did you meet him," I asked. "We met when I went hiking and I got stuck on a ledge and he helped me. I was hiking alone, which was stupid and so was he. We hiked to the top together after he rescued me and we talked for hours and we have been together ever since."

"I'm so happy for you Kate. When can I meet him," I asked. "When I get home, mom's having him over for dinner so we could meet." "I'm so excited for you," giggling like a school girl." "Do you think he's the one Kate?" "Yes, I really do," she smiled. "How's the sex," I asked. Shyly, she replied, "Amazing." We both laughed together and we had to get ready for dinner with Jonathon and his parents.

Kate was wearing a simple black dress and sandals. With her blonde hair and perfect body, she looked stunning. She helped me put my dress on and I had to ask her to leave for a minute, she didn't know that I was putting in my balls. She came back when I was done and said I looked beautiful in my favorite color of lavender.

We were meeting at Ceres Bistro for dinner, a fancy steakhouse, this was the night before Jon's graduation and his parents wanted to treat him to the best. Kate and I walked in and told the host we were with the Sears party, she walked us over where Jonathon, his mom and dad were sitting. The dining room was softly lit and there were chandeliers hanging over every table. The decor was beautiful and the aromas coming from the kitchen were even better. Kate and I got to the table and Jonathon and his father stood up. Jonathon was wearing black pants, a white shirt, black tie and a tan suit coat, he was delicious and my body starting tingling at the site of him.

Jonathon introduced Kate to his parents and we took our seats, me, seated next to Jon and Kate on the other side. Jon's mom was very cold to me but she seemed to like Kate, they were talking a lot. All I know is that she makes me very uncomfortable. Jonathon's dad was very friendly and told me I looked beautiful and Jon agreed and kissed my hand. They ordered a bottle of Dom to celebrate Jon's graduation and his mom said a toast:

"Jonathon, you have made me so proud, I wish you the best in your career path and I think at this time in your life, you should be single, here's to you," mom toasted. I could not believe she said this. "Why, Mrs. Sears, do you feel he should be single," I blurted out. "Brooke, I didn't mean anything toward you in particular. I think Jonathon has to be focused and cannot have distractions while interviewing and moving into his professional life."

Jonathon piped up, finally, "Mom, I love you and I understand where you're going with this, but Brooke is part of my life and I want her with me on this new journey." Mr. Sears told his wife to stop being so protective and let the boy enjoy his life, it was very uncomfortable and Kate sat silent. We ended the conversation and I found myself glaring at Mrs. Sears, I know she doesn't like me, I'm just not sure why.

Kate asked Jonathon about his speech he was giving at the ceremony as Valedictorian. He was excited about it and said, "It came out perfect I think, I hope." We can't wait to hear it Jonathon." Our dinners had arrived and I could barely eat, Jon put his hand under the table and I pushed it away, I was not in the mood. The rest of the dinner went okay, Kate was taking over the conversation, as Jon knew I was upset and remained quiet as well.

The Sear's picked up the tab and I whispered to Jon, "I have something for you; I want to give it to you tonight, before graduation." "We can walk home and have some time alone before the craziness of tomorrow and you can give it to me then," Jonathon smiled. I told Kate that I would meet her back at my room that I was going to walk home and Jon told his parents that he would see them tomorrow.

I graciously thanked Mr. and Mrs. Sears for dinner and Jon and I left the restaurant hand in hand, I could feel I was being stared at from behind, I turned my head back and his mother was nearly frothing at the mouth watching us walk out. This isn't good, I was thinking, his mother hates me.

We got outside and I lost it. Jon wiped my tears, "That's just my mother; she's very protective of me." "No, Jonathon, that woman hates me; she's made that much clear." "My mother doesn't hate anyone Brooke." "Well I'm the first then. Can we not talk about that right now Jon? This is really hard for me and I just want to be with you," I said wiping the tears away. He agreed and led me toward the park.

"The Weeping Willow Tree, how did you know I wanted to go here Jon?" "Like I said before, I know a lot about you," he grinned. "At least it's warm tonight." This is the perfect place to give him his new watch. I hope he loves it as much as I do. Ducking my head down to go under the hanging willows, a myriad of emotions came rushing to me. Memories of our night here and the night I came by myself to hide from life and it seems almost like good-bye tonight under this tree. He took my chin, looked in my eyes, and said, "This is our place Brooke, and we'll come back and visit over the years." Powerful words, I thought over the years.

He sat down next to me and I got the box out of the bag that I brought. He loved presents. He was so excited, that little boyish look again. I handed it to him, he tried to guess what it was, and he failed. "Just open it; you will never guess what's inside." He opened one box…nothing and then the next and saw the small box inside, he laughed at how I reproduced what he did for me at Christmas.

He opened the box and I had written a note on top:

My Jon,
This watch is a symbol of our time together and our future. Each time you look at the time, know that wherever I am, I am thinking of you. You are my love and I never want our clock to stop ticking.
Yours, Brooke

He kissed me passionately and said, "I love you Brooke Walsh." "Take the watch out Jon and turn it over." He took the watch out of its box and turned it over, the inscription said, Kudos, I am yours…Brooke, he sat silent. "Jonathon, what is it, do you not like it," I asked, with fear in my voice.

"Brooke, I love it and I'm overwhelmed by your thoughtfulness and kindness. You love me so much and I don't deserve it. It's moments like this that I know that I'm the luckiest guy in the world to have you in my life. You make me better or at least I try to be better, you make me believe I can do and be anything I want to be. Brooke, I was never looking for a partner because I know how fucked up I am and I didn't know how to handle love, until you. You have given me hope and trust that I can be the man you deserve and that I want to be for you. You comfort me even when I'm the one that has wronged; you love me when I don't deserve it. You make me laugh like no other, you're the girl I never thought I could have in my life, because of what and who I am. You have taught me so much and given me more than I could probably ever give you." When he stopped talking, he kissed me tenderly and whispered, "Kudos forever."

"Wait, listen to me, you have given me more than you know. You're my true first, you're my first love, and you're the first guy that ever gave me an orgasm. Remember you're the first one that ever said, 'I Love You' to me besides my dad and brother. You have taught me that I'm strong and courageous. You have made me feel beautiful, sexy, horny and loved. You haven't deprived me of anything. You are my choice forever. You are a good man, it has taken some stripping of some layers, but I found you and I believe in you."

We both sat under this tree and had tears, but we were happy. This moment was full of love and hope and I wished it could be frozen in time. "Jonathon, I want to make love to you, here, now, under our Willow Tree." Ever so gently, he pulled my spaghetti straps down, kissing my shoulders and my body was sizzling with love and desire. He pulled on my string and removed the Ben Wa Balls, this night, I wanted him and only him inside of me, to be one on this beautiful night, our last night here. I couldn't get enough of his kisses and his body against mine. He was gorgeous and this was beautiful, two people completely in love. I unzipped his pants, kissed the head of him, and brought him into me. It was different tonight; it was passionate and more intimate than ever before. I moved my hips to lock him in place and we both came together. He lay on top of me for quite some time after and we held each other close and produced more tears.

"I'll never forget this night, Jonathon Sears, it was

magical, you are magical and you're mine." "You're mine Brooke Walsh, all mine," he whispered in my ear. We headed on back to our walk home and he said he was going to talk to his mom and set her straight. That made me very happy. "She'll grow to love you Brooke, I promise." We got to my dorm and he walked me to the door. We kissed as if it was our last kiss and said goodnight. I wished him great success with his speech in the morning and he walked down the driveway as I watched him.

I wasn't the only one watching him, Steph was watching from her window, I yelled to him and told him to look up and he shot her the finger. It was yet another prefect ending to a perfect night. I went upstairs and Kate was already sleeping. I was happy because I didn't want to talk about his parents or anything, I just wanted to be in the moment that he and I just shared. I crawled in a sleeping bag that Pam lent me and fell right asleep.

"To all my fellow students, the faculty, our parents and siblings and Dean Frost, I would like to welcome you all here on this beautiful morning. Today is a day not about endings but about beginnings. Each of you sitting before us and me, will be walking out of here today. Some with a clear path to follow and some with uncertainty. No matter what your path may be, if you have love in your heart, no matter what that path, it will bring success to you."

"I stand here today looking around at all of you and I see such success awaiting you all, but I also see

familiar faces that through the last four years, I have wronged. My heart apologizes. These last four years have been a gift to all of us, we have all made good friends and hopefully have learned lessons and how to be strong on our own two feet in the real world."

"If you can leave today, remembering this, I will have done what I intended: We all have limited time on this earth to fulfill our hopes and dreams. I ask of you to live your own life and do not let others make choices for you; don't waste time because time is precious."

"Change is the opening for greatness and without it, we cannot become better, don't fear it, this is just another step on the journey to your life. Remember, the past is just that, past, it cannot be changed or tweaked, and it is finished. Your future is what matters and how you live it is your choice, but in those choices and decisions you make in your life, remember, you are the only one that is responsible for them, so choose them wisely."

"In closing, I would like to say...Don't ever be afraid to dream, but you must always be aware when your dreams have come true. Don't fear them; don't change them when they come, for they were your dreams to begin with. So I leave this great University with appreciation of all that it has taught me and all of you."

"It is my pleasure to share with you that I know I am already on the right path. May you all find yours and never look back. Congratulations to all of you and remember, with love, you can achieve anything."

The crowd roared when Jonathon finished his speech and tears were falling from all faces. I'm so proud of him and his words spoke volumes. Kate turned to me and said, "I think he was talking about you the whole time." "I doubt it, but I do hope that he really meant what he said, it was beautiful and inspiring."

After the ceremony was complete, Kate and I walked out of the stadium and Mrs. Sears came to me and said, "I'm so sorry for being rude to you, what Jonathon said up there today, he was talking about you, I can't deny him his happiness and from the sounds of it, you are his happiness." "Thank you Mrs. Sears, for that. As Jonathon said in his speech, we have to live our own lives and make our own choices, decisions and that is the single thing that prevents regret and resentment. With all due respect, Mrs. Sears, Jonathon is a grown boy and I believe he is mature enough to make his own decisions," I smiled and walked away.

Jonathon found Kate and I through the crowd and we both high fived him for an awesome speech. We took pictures and we headed back to my dorm to load the last things and be on our way home. Jon was staying one more night here to close up the frat house for his last time. I was driving back tomorrow with a U-Haul for all of his things to move to his parent's house for now.

We packed the last box in the van, turned around, said good-bye to my dorm and of course my friends with promises to stay in touch. I backed out of the driveway for thankfully my final time and saw Steph getting in her car; I smiled to her and drove behind Kate to the highway. Passing by the fraternity, I felt calmness come over me that I would never have to go in there again; I could leave the bad behind here. It's all a new from here.

When I arrived home, I was happy to be there. Kate and I unloaded my car and the van and I went to my room and just be. Something felt different to me, I cannot put my finger on it, but something is different. I sat on my beanbag and thought about Jon.

That first night we met and how he made my legs shake, laughing all night about our childhoods, him tying me up and leaving me there while he went to class, thankfully he locked the door. What a whirlwind, the log cabin, Christmas with my family and of course the Willow Tree. I missed him now more than ever. Have to write in my journal.

June 20
Will we make it with the distance? I really hope I am enough for him as Steph said I wasn't. I think we will, I pray we do. I really want to marry him. I never want to be without him, he is my soul mate.

I have to trust in us. I try to forget all that has gone bad, I forgive, but how can I forget. Will time heal that too? Who knows? For now, today, I am happy and in love. His mother is another story. Something about her, I don't trust. His father is awesome. I guess I can't change everyone......Until next time.

I went and picked up the U-Haul and headed back to campus to pick up Jonathon and all of his things. I'm not looking forward to seeing his mother; she really rubs me the wrong way. I know this could be a potential problem because Jon loves his mom as he should, but she doesn't like me, this I know. The good thing is we aren't staying there. We're unpacking and heading up to the beach in Maine for the weekend at a family friend's place.

Suddenly, I have butterflies in my stomach as I turn down his street. He was, for the final time, sitting on the steps waiting for me as he usually did. He was wearing black running shorts and a red Nike t-shirt, with sunglasses on and he was smoking. I was wearing white shorts and a red tank top, and it was very hot outside. "Hey, who is that sexy girl in the U-Haul," he yelled to me. I laughed and said, "Hey do you need a lift?" "I think I'm getting one now seeing you in that big truck," he replied with a grin. "Such a pig at times," shaking my head.

Nate and two other assholes that were still at the house came down with some boxes and packed them in the truck. He didn't have nearly as many clothes as I, but he had his desk and his couch that were big. It took about an hour to load and Jon asked, "do you want to say good-bye to my room for one last time?" "No, I'm ready to forget that place." He needs not an explanation; he shook is friend's hands and got in the driver's seat of the U-Haul, and we were off, Good Fucking Riddance.

"Jon, I'm really uncomfortable with your mom. Did she tell you she spoke to me yesterday after graduation?" "No, she just said that you were a nice girl and you were growing on her." "Well, I'm glad that I'm growing on her, like a fungus," I sarcastically spoke. "What did she say to you," Jon asked. "She told me that she thought your speech was about me and that I make you happy." "Brooke, the speech was about you and to you. You have changed me Brooke Walsh," he said, reaching over and grabbing my hand.

There was no air-conditioning in the U-Haul and we were both sweating. Jon was driving too fast for my liking and I told him to slow down. He slowed all the way down and said, "How's this?" "What are you doing, you can't stop on a major highway Jonathon," I screamed. There were no windows in the back of the truck, so I couldn't see to his left. "We are in the breakdown lane silly," he smiled. "What for," I asked.

"I can't stand to see your wet spot between your legs from the sweat," he laughed. "Oh, I didn't know that was there, sorry," I blushed. "Don't be sorry, I love when you're wet and I want to make you even wetter in the back of this truck!" "We can't do that on a highway Jonathon, we'll get arrested." He put his hand up my shorts and the next thing I knew I was in the back of the truck. It was sweltering hot; there were boxes, a desk and a couch that was crowding all the space.

Boxes were tipping over as he put me on the couch. Brooke, I need to taste you, so I kissed him and he said, no, I need your other lips. His shorts were off and he was raging. "Jonathon, I want to taste you while you taste me," this was a first. He got on top of me, the opposite way and I took him in my mouth. His legs were shaking and his mouth was on fire, I wrapped my legs around his head and he licked harder until I couldn't hold back any longer. He turned me over and inserted himself in be from behind. The sweat was pouring off us; I nearly slipped off the couch. The truck was rocking. He went further and further in me until he literally screamed in pleasure.

We both felt like jelly now and couldn't move. We

thought we heard voices outside the truck so we hurried and put our clothes on and went back in the front. Thankfully, it must have been someone driving by with the radio. We laughed so hard and continued on our trip to his parent's house.

"Jon, would you still love me if we didn't have sex," I asked. "Why are you asking me this Brooke?" "I just want to know if I'm enough for you without it." "I would still love you, but not as deep as I do because there would still be things we didn't know about each other, plus the sex with you is incredible." "You've taught me everything, and I still have a lot to learn Jon. "I'll be your teacher," he laughed. "I'll be your student forever, but we have to stop talking like this because we must be close to your parents and I don't want to have to stop again and let you teach me."

"This weekend at the beach Brooke, I want you to tell me what you want and what you like and I will teach you anything you want to know." "So, you want my wish list Jon," I laughed. "Anything you desire is what you will get. Okay I can't get out of the car now. I'm stranded with a hard on. We have to wait, look the other way; this will stay hard if you look at me." We both cracked up laughing.

His mom is walking out to the car waving us to come in. Uggg, this had better be quick. Jon is back in his shorts and we can now get out and go inside. "How was the traffic Jon on the way down," his mom asked. "I didn't notice any traffic", he looked at me, and we laughed. "Brooke, how are you?" she asked. "I am great and yourself?" I replied. She said, "Better that my boy is home where he belongs." Jon reminded, "You remember mom that we're only here to drop things off, then we're heading up to Maine." She snarled and said, "Oh, I forgot."

I think this woman is in love with her own son. It's very creepy. His dad walked in and I was happy because he is much nicer to me. Jon and he gave handshakes and I went and helped them unload the truck, I didn't want to stay inside with his mom. She called to me and said, "Brooke, this is a man's job, come and sit on the deck with me and have some lemonade." I couldn't say no that would be rude, so I went and took a seat on the deck, I saw the woodpile and I felt dirty again. Mrs. Sears started asking me questions that I wasn't prepared to answer.

"What do you plan on doing without Jonathon, you know, since you won't be living close by," she asked. "We're going to make it work; during the summer of course we'll see each other more than when I'm in school and when he gets a job." "Do you want to marry my son, Brooke," she asked. "Mrs. Sears, I'll be very honest with you, if he asked me to marry him today, I would say yes, I love him."

"He's not ready for marriage, he doesn't even have a job yet," she said so rude. "I know that, Mrs. Sears, but you asked me a question and I answered it honestly," saying as I'm getting pissed. "You are young Brooke. Don't you think you need to experience more before you think about marriage," she said. "Do you mean be with other men or what does that mean," I asked. "What I mean Brooke; I don't think you're mature enough yet to be in a serious relationship with my son. He has so much that he needs to do with his career and such and I don't want him to miss out on anything because you're in his life." "Mrs. Sears, you're his mother and he loves you very much, but as I told you at graduation, he makes his own decisions and if he chooses to be with me, there is not a damn thing you can do about it," I snickered. My hands are shaking and I have to get the fuck out of here, "Please excuse me, I'm going to see if they need help."

Out to the truck I went to tell Jon we needed to hurry up and leave. He knew I was on the deck with his mom and figured that is what got me upset. "What did she say to you?" he asked. "Jon I think you should ask her yourself. I just want to leave." "No, we're not leaving until I settle this once and for all." He brought the last box in the house and told his mom and dad to come in the living room.

I sat on the footstool while Jon sat in the chair right behind me and his mom and dad sat across from us on the couch. Jonathon said, "Mom, do you see this girl in front of me?" "Yes." "Good, because this is the girl I love mom and you can't change that."

"Why would I want to do that," she asked all innocently? "You've said some pretty mean things to Brooke and I want it to stop now." His dad sat silently.

"You have no idea mom what this girl has done for me. She has given me confidence that I never had. She has enabled me to dream again and to believe there's nothing I can't do. She loves me with all that she is and she has made me a better person; so why the hell would you want to break that up?" "Jonathon, she wants to marry you. She told me earlier. I know she's going to try and trap you."

"Mrs. Sears, you asked me if I wanted to marry your son and I said, if he asked me I would say yes. I never said that without you prompting me too." His dad chimed in and said, to his wife, "These kids are happy and in love, let them be." "Jonathon, you have a bright career ahead of you; you can't be distracted by a college sweetheart. "Mom, this conversation is over and we are leaving. I'll call you after the weekend," he said and grabbed my hand and we walked out.

"Boy Darlene, you really know how to make people feel warm and fuzzy," Ed Sears said to his wife. "You know how broken hearted he was before; after him and Steph broke up." "That was a long time ago. Can't you see he is happy now and let it be," he yelled at her! "Plus, that was high school and he is grown up now," he said to his wife." "Steph was strong and she is a go-getter. This girl, she looks weak and dependent. I don't like her." "Well, you don't have to sleep with her. It is his choice Darlene. The sooner you realize that, the better off we will all be." "I will not accept this; he knows what he has to do and who he has to be with. His dreams will be shattered if he stays with Brooke," Darlene shouted. "His dreams are his dreams Darlene and if they change, that is because he wants them to change."

"Ed, I'm his mother and I know what he wants and she isn't it. You know he wants to have money we never had. You know he has always dreamt about owning his own engineering firm. She will take that away from him and I will not stand and support it," she said.

"I'm so sorry. Don't listen to her; she doesn't know you like I do Brooke." "It hurts Jon; I want her to like me because that will ultimately affect us down the road." "Don't worry about her Brooke; what matters is that I love you and you love me back. Just sit back and start thinking about your wish list," he chuckled trying to lighten the mood.

We finally got to the U-Haul place to return the truck and get my car. "Only an hour and half to Maine, I can't wait to get there and ride the trolley and make sundaes with you Jon," I smiled. "You are so damn cute Brooke Walsh." "I think I'm going to try and sleep. I think I'll need all my energy for later," I chuckled. "You sleep my dirty girl, you sleep."

He woke me up when we passed over the bridge so I could see the big Tuna that was just caught and brought in. It had to weigh 1000 lbs. "Did you have a nice nap," he asked. "Yes, it was wild, no tell, I'll show you later. See what you do to me Jonathon Sears, you make me think dirty thoughts and you make me want to act on them, that isn't like me." "Well, then I guess I've been a good teacher," he laughed.

We pulled into the cottage in Ogunquit and it was a mile away from the beach, but the Viking Ice cream was close so that made it just fine. There are many people staying here with only three bedrooms, so they set up tents in the back yard. We'll be sleeping in a tiny tent, should be fun. "Welcome," Sharon said, "so glad you two made it up here." My mom peeked around the corner and said, "Hey kids, you can put your things in the room I'm in." We got our things and dropped it in my mom's room.

"So, we'll be able to get in if we have to pee from the tent," I asked Sharon. "Of course, I've set them all up with pillows and blankets and the back door will be open all night." "Thank you Sharon and thanks for having us." "You are most welcome Brooke and it's nice that you both could come." "Do you have anything planned for this evening you two?" Jon and I looked at each other, "we sure do."

We walked down to the trolley stop and waited for it to come by and bring us down to the cove to get candy. We put our quarters in and sat in the back of the trolley. In the back of the trolley there was no cover, we were enjoying the breeze. Jon held my hand and kissed me. He whispered to me, you're my wish list." How can it be possible to love him more than I do, but somehow I just do. The trolley stopped and we got out at the Cove and went in the penny candy store. Swedish fish, pixy styx, pop rocks, bottle caps, rock candy and so much more, we grabbed a bag and filled it with our favorites. It was so fun and juvenile. A new trolley came and we got back on to go build our own sundae at the Viking, my favorite place to go when I come here.

I asked Jon, "What's your favorite ice cream flavor?" "You!" "Seriously, what is it?" "Pistachio Nut and yours?" "The same." "Wow, I never knew that, what a coincidence." We kept smiling at each other. We got off the trolley and skipped into the Ice Cream place, there was whipped cream, gummy worms, Oreo cookies, white chocolate, hot fudge, butterscotch and at least 30 more items to pack on our sundaes.

Jon ordered a small because he said he didn't want to get full, his real dessert was coming next. He is gluttonous for sex. I ordered a small as well and we fed each other bites so we could taste as many toppings. We had so much fun; I'm excited to go down to the beach now. I hope the beach is empty because I have a wish list that I need to collect.

We walked down to the beach, I knew of a place

that was like a cave, with rocks on 3 sides and an opening. I had to bring him there. We used to come here as a family every year, so I'm very familiar with the right places. My sisters and brother and I used to play hide in seek and this was the place I always hid. It's completely secluded and private.

It was dark and damp in this sea cave. I'm nervous; I don't have much of a wish list. There is one thing I know he'll love, but I'm a bit scared and uncomfortable about it. Right now, I wish I were drunk.

"So, my dirty girl, what's on your wish list," Jon asked. "Jonathon, I'm nervous. I want to please you so bad and be unforgettable to you, but I don't know if I can do it." "Do what?" "I can't even say it." "Don't be nervous Brooke, it's just you and me and we don't have to do anything you don't want to do, come and sit with me," he pulled me down on his lap.

"If we just sat here in each other's arms all night looking out at the ocean beyond that opening, it would be just fine with me babe." "Really Jon?" "I would love that, but you just put me in a trance and I want more. I want to be your student Jonathon; I just don't want to fail." "There is no way you could fail, your grades have been A's thus far," he said with a smile.

I turned around and I straddled him. I kissed him and he responded with passion and thrusting from below. "Brooke, we're here on this beautiful beach, the waves are crashing in front of us and I want to please you, tell me what you want. I will do anything you want," he moaned, while twirling my hair. "I want you in every way possible Jon." I had to be memorable to him; I had to be enough for him that's all that's going through my mind. I had to be more than Steph, whatever that even means.

"Tell me what you like, what makes you feel good babe?" Shyly, "I like when you lick me, your tongue is so soft and talented." "You like that ha, when I taste you and put my tongue inside you? Good, because I love to lick and kiss you, you taste so sweet." "Wait," I said and poured pixy stix down my body for him to lick off me. He started from my left breast and moved over to the right and down to my belly button. He licked and sucked the sugar out as my body responded with shivers. The good kind of shivers, the ones you can feel all through your body. He grazed his mouth lower and created an explosion in me that mimicked that first night. Once catching my breath, I turned over and said, "It's time for me to let you teach me." Nothing could be more intimate and personal than what he just did to me this shouldn't be so bad. He had always said he wanted to leave nothing to the imagination, so this is the last of it.

"What do you want me to teach you my dirty girl?" "I want you in my ass Jon." He was elated, instant hard on. He pulled me up on all fours and he slowly entered my backside, it was uncomfortable at first, but he was panting and I knew he was enjoying it. He massaged my nipples, moaned and fell on top of me breathless.

"Now, you've had all of me Jonathon." "You're all that I want Brooke, not only do you make me happy, but you satisfy me in every way. You have earned an A+ in my class," he laughed. "That wasn't my favorite position, but I wanted you to have all of me. Let's not make that a habit, okay." "Whatever you desire, is my command," he kissed my mouth.

Wiping the sand and sugar off, we decided the ocean was where we needed to rinse off. We ran down the beach naked and jumped in the waves. The moon was bright, the stars were out and we had this infinite ocean to ourselves. I had another first with him tonight and everything felt right in the world. We jumped waves, held on together, and floated until we both got cold, so we went back in the cave and got dressed.

"Jon, what do you think about staying here all night?" "Let's do it, this is an amazing night Brooke, I love your passion." "I have always wanted to sleep in this little cave as a kid and now, it's even better than I imagined, here with you," I whispered. This night couldn't be more perfect. With the salty smell of the ocean, the sound of the waves and my beautiful man beside me, satisfying my every need. Perfection!

We lay in the sand, which was now stuck to our wet bodies, and cuddled. I feel like I'm in a dream and I never want to wake from it. He and I were on our sides, he was staring into my eyes, and it sent chills down my spine. "What are you thinking about Jonathon? "The thought of you with another guy makes me crazy; promise me, you'll never do it."

"Jonathon, why are you thinking that?" "You know I would never cheat on you and I don't want or love anyone but you." "Brooke, to be honest, I'm scared that we're going to be living in different states and I know we all have needs." "Jonathon, I need nothing but you, I don't need sex, only with you. I want you forever please never doubt that." "I can't get the thought of you being in the same town with Josh out of my mind." I sat up and blurted, "If you really think that I'm that desperate to have sex if we're apart a few days, than you don't know me very well after all. I have no feelings for Josh, he was a high school mistake, and you are the real love of my life Jon."

"I have given you all of me, nothing left to the imagination now Jon and I want to be your forever. No matter what happens down the road, that's what I will be. You need to start believing in my love. Why do you doubt it?" "I was hurt before Brooke, I never told you about it before," he blurted out. "Did she cheat on you Jon," I asked. "Yes, with a good friend of mine." "Was it Rick?" "No, it was Robby, him, Rick and I were best of friends all through grade school and high school." "I'm so sorry Jon, I know the feeling and it sucks."

"It was after that, I started to not connect with girls and I just fucked them, no strings, no nothing. I wanted to punish every girl until you." Things were starting to make more sense to me now. I felt for him, whoever this bitch was that deceived him was to blame for his behaviors. "Jon, it's me and I would never do that to you and I never want to be with another guy for the rest of my life, you are the only one for me." I reached across to him and pulled him in for a big hug.

He grabbed the back of my head in an instant, started kissing my mouth with force. He pushed himself inside me hard, harder and harder, it hurt, and brought tears to my eyes. As much as I didn't like it like that, I knew he needed this to feel more in control of his life and his feelings. When we were finished, I told him I was his and to never doubt that again. "Jonathon, you don't have to worry, maybe you've never had love like this before and neither have I, but we have to trust this." He pulled me close to him and rested my head on his chest and we fell asleep in the sand.

The sun came up and we were still in the cave, covered in sand. The smell of the ocean and the sound of the seagulls were incredible to wake to. He looked at me and said, "Good morning my girl." "Good morning to you, my man. I hope that you slept well and you feel better this morning." "I feel much better and thank you for last night, I really needed it." "I love you more than anything in this world Jonathon; oceans cannot keep my love away from you." He gave me a huge smile and a hug that wasn't releasing.

We had to get back to the cottage before they found out we were missing. We hopped on the trolley and headed back up to town to the cottage. We tried to sneak in the back, but my mom caught us and said, "Where have you kids been all night?" "Mom, we fell asleep on the beach," smiling to Jon. "To be young again," mom rolled her eyes. We were starving and we could smell bacon cooking from inside and we went in and ate. After breakfast, we went for a long walk on the Marginal Way before we headed back to my house.

We didn't talk much on our walk; we were taking in the scenery and enjoying being together. Up high above the ocean, it was a place where all dreams were possible. We sat down on the rocks and I asked Jon, "Where do you want to work?" "Well, I've been sending resumes out and I'm hoping I'll hear from this huge engineering firm in Connecticut." His face lit up when he talked about it and he said, "The opportunities are plenty there and they are a solid company, it's always been my dream job." "If that's your dream job, you'll get it; just believe as I believe in you. Connecticut, Jonathon, that's two hours away from me." A pit has now formed in my stomach.

"I know it's a drive, but this is my future and this is where I want to go." "Well, we'll just have to do a lot of traveling, won't we? You better get yourself a better car that's more reliable," I laughed. "If I get this job, I'll be able to afford to buy one." "So, that means you won't be living with your mom, so that's a plus," I said happily. "My mom is harmless Brooke; don't worry about her."

"Let's get going back to my house Jon; I just want to lay low before you head back home." He gave me a piggy bag the rest of the way and we went and said thank you and good-bye. In the car, we were figuring out how we were going to see each other if he got the job in Connecticut. I wanted him to get the job, it was his dream job, after all, but a part of me was unsure he was going to handle the distance. Right now, we can only concentrate on the now and that's what I plan to do.

"Home sweet home, we have the house all to ourselves. Mom is still in Maine and dad is on business in Delaware". We walked in the house and my cat greeted us, Jon didn't like cats, but that was something he had to get used to because I love them. He went and sat on the couch and turned the TV on and I was going through the mail to see if I got my grades. There it was...My transcripts, "Jon, they're here, my grades," I nervously said. "What are you waiting for, open them!" "I'm scared," I admitted. He got up and took the envelope and opened it for me and hugged me so tight and said, "I'm so proud of you Brooke Walsh, I told you, you were an A student." "What!" I shouted, "Did I do it?" "Yes, you did my girl, a 4.0!" "Oh my god, I can't believe it! Thank you so much!" I kissed him and then danced around the kitchen.

There was another package for me, but it has no return address, so I opened it and dropped it to the floor. "What is it," Jon asked. He picked it up off the floor, looked at it, and almost died. I ran and locked myself in my room and wouldn't let him in. After a half an hour, he pushed the door so hard that he loosened the chair I had put in front and he got in. "Brooke, let me explain."

"This was from High School." "I thought you only had one–nighters with her Jon," I cried out. "We did, when I first came to college." "So Amazon Steph was the fucking girl that broke your heart?" "Yes, Brooke, I'm sorry I didn't tell you, I just couldn't." "So that explains it all Jon. That's why she made my life miserable and tried to break us up because she wants you back." "Brooke, she turned psycho after I broke up with her. After that, she enrolled at the same college without me knowing. I'll admit and I'm not proud but there were some drunken lonely nights that I did go to her, but they meant nothing. I only wanted to punish her."

"In this picture Jon, you two look happy and she was actually pretty then." "We were happy and young then, she was my first." "I'm going to throw up!" "It was puppy love, what we have is real and forever, there is no comparison. You were in love with Josh before me. We both have a past Brooke."

"Why would she send this picture to me?" "Brooke she wants me back. She'll do anything to break us up, she is insane. She'll never get me back; I love you and only you." "Did your mom like her?" "My mom loved her," sorry to say. You have to understand, we were young and she was a sweet girl then. She snapped after we broke up. She has shown her true colors, she's unstable." "Jon, I can't compete with that and you know it," I cried. "Brooke, this is my life and my mother can't tell me who I can date and who I can't. Steph was in the past and there is where she will stay," he said trying to grab me in a hug.

"So, this is your picture? I see the writing on it. How did she get it?" "It was in a box in my room at school from freshman year. I have no idea how she got it." Then it dawned on me, Noelle and she were in conspiracy mode in that note I read and they were going to exchange goods and Noelle must have found this and fucking gave her my address. "I need to sleep and stop my mind Jon, this is a lot for me to take in and I'm really not feeling well." "Can I sleep next to you babe?" "Yes, sleep, but nothing else."

I lie there facing the wall, with tears running down my face and he's spooning me from behind. Steph was right, she had him first and she had something I could never give him. Why would he lie to me about her, what else is he hiding? This is worse for me than everything else he has done, this bitch made my life hell. He did tell her though there would never be a "them" that day at her dorm, maybe he really is over her. She's the reason he thinks I will cheat, she's the reason for all of his desperate lovemaking. He must have really loved her.

Jon got out of bed and went down to the kitchen and tried to make me some soup, he knows I say it is the cure all. I could smell it and I woke up and went downstairs. He was on the couch crying in his hands. He looked up and said to me, "I hate her, I really hate her," My response was, "Well love and hate are very close relatives, are you sure it's hate and not love?" "I love you and only you, please know that," he pleaded. "I thought you did but that was a pretty big lie Jonathon, under the circumstances," I said. "I'm sorry, I didn't want to lose you or hurt you by telling you, I was trying to protect you," he said.

"Is she out of your life now Jonathon?" "Yes, I haven't been with her since freshman year, she has stalked me and begged me, but I refused her over and over. Can we forget about her and just enjoy being together?" "For now, I can push it back, but I won't forget Jon."

"Jonathon, I really don't feel well." "Brooke, you need to eat some soup, you even say it's a cure all." "It was very sweet of you to make this for me, but I don't think I can eat right now, I think I am going to get my period."

"Well, it's there for you when you're ready," and he pulled me into an embrace. "Why does loving you have to hurt so much, it's so intense, as if it can explode at any second." He got silent and sat down. He was thinking about something; I could feel it.

"I have to call my mom," he said, if he didn't she would torture him when he got home. He picked up the phone and called her and she said, "I have a surprise for you when you get home." "I can only imagine mom. I'll be home in the morning; I have a lot of calls to make for an interview." "Drive safe sweetheart and remember what you have ahead of you." He rolled his eyes and hung up the phone. "Was your mom upset you were staying with me tonight?" "Forget about her, I want to make you feel better babe."

"Come over here and lay down so I can make you all better," he waved me over. I lay across his lap and he massaged my belly, but his hands started to wander and he was quickly cupping my vagina. Why? Why can I not resist him? Why does he get me every time, he upsets me and I'm an idiot and I want him more? "Don't move Brooke. Let me feel you." As if for the last time, he was rubbing, touching, kissing every orifice of my body, sensually, gently, kind, and I could stand it no more and he brought me to complete ecstasy, again. "Your body Brooke is so soft and beautiful and when you move your body with mine, you bring me to new dimensions. Just like this Brooke, inside as I grind more into you, you move to lock me in and I'm trapped in you and in your love, this is my favorite place to be, "he said softly.

"Do you feel any better now?" "In some ways, yes and others not, but your touch makes me feel good always. I'm ready for some soup; let's see how yours compares Jon." He nervously walked over and poured some in a bowl for me. "Not bad, Jonathon, not bad, another secret you're just revealing," I laughed. "Soup and you are all I need." "Then that's what it will be tonight babe."

We watched movies, cuddled, and slept off and on through the night. We woke up in the morning and Jonathon had to get back home to set up for interviews. Something is telling me this is good-bye, not a see you soon. "Jonathon, thank you for teaching me so much, thank you for teaching me what I want and don't want in a lover. Thank you for loving me the way you have and thank you for making me bathe in your beauty this long." "It sounds like you're saying good-bye, Brooke. This isn't good-bye; this is only the beginning of our lives together. Please know that Steph is in the past, you and I are the future."

He hugged me tight and kissed me and we headed out to get his rental car. I was quiet the whole ride there and I was afraid to let him out of the car, fearing this was it. I begged him to stay, but I knew he had to go, he had a dream to fulfill and I couldn't get in his way. He picked out a Mustang convertible so he could be cool on the way home; he was so damn sexy in it. "Jonathon, I love you and I'll miss you, don't forget to call me," I said through my tears. "Brooke, I love you and I'll see you soon, Kudos," and he kissed me softly. I smiled and off he drove

Mom and dad came home tonight and we had a simple dinner together, it was nice. They were grilling me about Jonathon, in this moment, I felt like I wanted to die. Unrelenting fear that it was over engulfed me and I knew when he was home with his mom, something would change him. I told mom and dad

things were fine and he was setting up interviews and he'd be very busy. Mom knew something was wrong, but I couldn't express it with accuracy.

"Brooke, honey, he has to move toward his future, the distance and time will tell if you are truly meant to be together. If it doesn't, it was never meant to be," mom said. Only my mom could say that without me punching her at this time. "I know mom, I'm just scared and his mom hates me. I know she's going to sabotage us." "Brooke, she doesn't know you and I bet she's afraid you're going to take her son away from her. I'm sure she's scared because anyone who sees the two of you together knows you are in love." "Really mom, do you really think so?" "Yes, honey I do." "Mom, you always know how to make me feel better, I love you."

The phone rang at 10:31am and it was Jonathon. "Hello," "I got it, I got the interview Brooke," he said excitedly. "Oh Jonathon, I'm so happy for you, when is it," I asked. "Tomorrow at 9am, I'm heading there tonight and going to stay in a hotel," he said. A hotel without me, my stomach churned. "Don't worry, you'll be with me. I stole a picture of you off the mantel," he laughed. "You did, well I guess that's the next best thing."

"You're going to do great! Make sure you wear that black suit I love, it makes you look like God," I laughed. He laughed back. "Okay, I have to go get things ready; will call you tonight, kudos." "Kudos to you, love ya."

Connecticut, hmmm, good for him, bad for us, I thought, trying to replay my mom's words in my mind, "If it's meant to be it will be". Shopping is the answer; I need to shop to feel better. Got in my car and headed to the mall, but I suddenly wasn't feeling well again. I must be getting my period; I had to turn around and go lay down. I slept for hours and took a shower to see if that would help the cramps, but no relief.

At 9:15 pm, the phone rang and it was Jonathon, he had arrived at the hotel. "Hey my girl, how are you?" "Not feeling well, but I'm fine. Are you ready for the interview?" "Ready as I'll ever be." "Are you going to wear the black suit?" "Yes and my watch, so I know you'll be with me." "I'm always with you Jonathon. Get some sleep and good luck; let me know how it goes." "I will and remember Brooke; I love you to the moon and back." "Right back at you Jonathon." We hung up and my stomach was queasy thinking about the distance that will be between us.

He got the job and he was moving to Connecticut. He was staying with a friend while looking for an apartment. One of his fraternity brothers got a job at the same place and they were renting a house together. He was excited and I for him, but selfishly wishing he was closer.

He was starting the new job the next Monday so I was driving to Connecticut Friday to help domesticate his new place. I'm excited to see his new place and actually happy he's no longer at this mom's house. I'm bringing him some pictures of us that I had framed and some plants for his new place and some food. I made him some muffins and cookies and a meatloaf to freeze and some spaghetti sauce, at least enough to get him started.

The ride is long and I can't wait to get there and see his face. I miss him so much. After the two-hour drive, I have arrived. What a cute little white cape, with dark green shutters. There's a small yard in front up on a hill with beautiful flowers blooming and the back yard was tiny with a birdbath and a picnic table.

He met me at the door, picked me up, and then carried me over the threshold. He made me feel special and it was very cute. The inside needed a woman's touch and the kitchen was very small. He gave me the tour, a living room, and kitchen and bathroom on the first floor and upstairs there were two bedrooms and a bathroom. It was perfect, actually for two guys to share.

He had my photo set up right by his bed on the nightstand. It warmed my heart. "This is really cute Jonathon." He was happy, I could tell. "It won't be complete until I have you in my bed Brooke." "I won't argue with you sir; your wish is my command." He pushed me down on the bed and slammed into me so hard and I had to stop him and ask him," What are you doing?" "I need you; I need to feel you deep." He didn't stop, he came, and he got right up, put his pants back on, and went downstairs.

What just happened, I was thinking to myself, he just completely fucked me and walked away. I stayed in the bed and he came up to get me a half hour later. "Hey, I thought you were going to put a woman's touch to this place?" He was acting as if nothing was wrong. "I'll be right there," and followed him down the stairs. Maybe all was okay, but he's never just got up and walked away, not even on the first night. My gut feels like shit and I'm sensing something. I just went with the flow and started putting the food away that I brought and hung some pictures. My favorite picture was of him and me at the beach on the rocks holding hands; we stopped someone to snap the picture.

On the kitchen table, I placed a bamboo plant in the middle that I bought him and he had no idea what it was, "What is that plant?" "It's a bamboo plant, it's said to give luck, and I thought it was perfect for you." "I love it babe, thank you." He gave me a peck on the cheek and a smile. His mom had given him some curtains so we put them up and it made me think how much I didn't trust her. We dilly-dallied around for a while with little conversation, something has changed with him and I don't know what. I want to go home; I've never felt like this before with him.

His roommate came home and loved what I had done with the place. He was friendly enough, but I didn't feel comfortable at all there. "Jonathon, can I talk to you alone please," I asked. "Sure, let's go to my room." "I think I'm going home, something's really wrong here and I'm not feeling well Jon." He had the strangest look in his eyes, "You aren't feeling good again. Did you get your period yet?" "No, it's probably because of moving and such and not being with the same girls, my cycle must be off."

"I don't want you to leave. Why would you want to leave, we've been apart long enough?" "Why did you just fuck me like that Jonathon," I asked, and now tears are flowing. "I told you Brooke, I needed to be deep in you, I missed you, I needed it, and I needed you." "You got up and left me right after, like I was some tramp or something Jonathon." "Don't ever talk about yourself like that," he scowled at me. "Then don't treat me like that and I won't feel like that."

"Please stay, I want to wake up next to you in the morning. I want to feel your heart beating. I want to know you are mine, I need that Brooke, please," he begged. "Fine, I will stay," I said and he smiled and kissed my nose. "I want to take you to dinner and a movie tonight, what would you like to see?" "How about 'Fatal Attraction' with Michael Douglas?" "Oh yeah, I heard it was a great movie, Fatal Attraction it is babe."

"Can I take a shower," I asked him. "Yes, the cold is the hot and the hot is the cold, so be careful, laughing, it's not the Ritz, but it'll do." I went in the shower and prayed he wouldn't come in with me. I needed think of what could be going on with him. Why he is acting so out of sorts and desperate. Walking out of the bathroom, I heard him on the phone, he was angry and he hung up on whoever it was. "Jonathon is everything okay," I yelled to him. "Yes, fine, telemarketer."

He came up the stairs and as I was drying off, he took the towel from me, I was naked, standing in his room and he was looking at me up and down and said, "I need to make love to you, I need to make up for earlier, plus you didn't even come Brooke, I can't have that." "Jonathon, I just took a shower." "I know, that's when you're the sweetest tasting," he whispered as he sucked my ear.

"I can't get enough of you Brooke, please let me please you." "You do please me Jonathon, what has gotten into you?" "You have. You brought me meals, pictures and plants. You're the kindest woman I have ever met and I want to repay you for your kindness," he then grazed my clit with his lips, still standing up; he was on his knees between my legs. He spread my legs apart and over his shoulders so he could put his tongue deep in me, it felt so good, he kept saying to me, "Come baby, come, show me you love me." He sucked everything out of me and I couldn't move. "That's my girl, you are all mine."

We ate dinner at this little Italian Restaurant, it was delicious, the conversation was good, but something was still not right. Maybe it was PMS for me and I was over analyzing, I'm not sure. We waited in line for popcorn at the movies and then went and sat in the highest seats possible. I want to be as alone as possible in here with you," he whispered. The movie was crazy and I had to grip his hands a few times. It was nice though, being together like a normal couple. After the movie, we went back to his place and went to sleep, at least I tried to fall asleep, and I didn't feel well again. I woke him up and asked, "Can you rub my belly to help me fall asleep?" He reached his hands under the covers and gently rubbed my belly and then my hair and we both fell asleep.

"I wish I could wake up next to you every morning Brooke." "Well, that can be arranged." "I wish it could, I really wish it could Brooke, that's what I want." "Me too, I can transfer somewhere here, you can go to work and I go to school and we could be together every day." "I couldn't have you do that now. You're so close to finishing up and that would put you behind." "It wouldn't put me far behind; it would be worth it Jonathon. I could take some classes at night too. I could make your mornings really good, Jon," I said with a smirk. "Brooke, I want that more than you know, but it's impossible. We have to wait." He's being evasive and it's scaring me a bit.

We made love; it was nice, soft and gentle. After we showered together, we stood under the stream of water and just held each other. We had a muffin together before I headed back home; I wanted him to have the day to prepare for his first day of work on Monday. Before leaving, I tidied up the house and pictured myself living here, with him. The simple thought made me happy. All of a sudden, the phone rang and he answered it, "Not now!" angrily, and hung up. "Those goddamn telemarketers, even on a Sunday they don't give you a break." "Hey, they're just doing their job cut them some slack." "Brooke, I don't know how you can always find the good in everything. I wish I was more like that." "It's all about choice Jon, all about choice."

I wanted to see what he was wearing on his first day of work before I left. He brought me up to his closet and had me pick it out for him. It reminded me of Pam and how she would do this with me, I miss her, I thought. One, two, three and oh, we cannot forget four, an off white pair of Chinos, a navy blue shirt and a pale yellow tie and underwear, "you have to wear underwear to work Jonathon." "It's not fair to me if you don't," he laughed and then I did, after hearing him laugh. "I love you Brooke Walsh, always know that no matter what." "I do know that Jonathon. Man, you're going to be one handsome dude at your new job; you better stay hidden from all the women co-workers." "Don't worry Brooke; I have the watch, so I know you're with me."

"Are you ready for the big day tomorrow," I asked. "I have a few things to do, but my outfit and underwear are ready, thanks to you," he said smiling.

"Will you walk me to my car? I should let you get your things done." He took my hand and walked me to my car. We kissed passionately. It felt final. I began to tear up and Jon noticed and said, "Why are you crying babe? "Jonathon, it just feels like this is good-bye." "Brooke, it will never be good-bye. Don't you worry yourself, I love you and only you." I hugged him again and got in my car. "Drive safe babe, I'll let you know how my first day goes, Kudos." "I'll be looking forward to hearing from you and how fabulous they think you are, Kudos."

Driving and thinking I just saw him for the last time. Something has changed and I have to throw up. I pulled over in the breakdown lane and threw up. I remember the breakdown lane with him, it felt much better than this. Is it over? Why do I feel like this? It has to be my hormones, I can't wait to get my period and think rationally. He said he loved me and he made love to me. Everything is fine; it has to be just me. I'm over thinking and all the changes are making me anxious. Everything is fine.

He called me after his first day of work and said it was a lot of meeting and introductions, but it was good. He sounded tired. I didn't want to keep him, he was probably hungry and I felt terrible. We said goodnight and I paused and asked, "Is everything okay?" "Everything is fine babe, I'm just overwhelmed." I could sense something wasn't right. "Okay, sleep well and make sure you eat dinner, I love you." "I love you too Brooke, more than anything."

The week went on with quick phone calls and no mention of weekend plans to see each other. I'm going to the doctor today to see why I feel so awful. Sitting on the table in the doctor's office with a paper covering over me, I began to panic about what could be wrong with me. The doctor came in, checked my blood pressure, pulse, and listened to my lungs and all were fine. She asked me about my symptoms and I told her I was very tired all the time, nauseous, vomiting and she smirked at me. She handed me a cup to pee in and led me to the bathroom.

I must have a Urinary Tract Infection, that's why I have to pee in the cup, I was thinking. I gave the nurse the cup, went back into the room, and waited for the doctor to come back in. The doctor came back in and read through my chart where it noted I was on birth control pills, she asked, "have you missed any of your pills?" "No, I'm positive, I'm very careful about that, why," I asked. "Brooke, you're pregnant," the doctor said. "What, that is impossible!" I yelled out, "I use protection." "Brooke it isn't 100%," she replied. A million things are now running through my mind, "I thought I was late for my period because of moving," I said. "No Brooke, you're pregnant," she repeated. "Do you know what you want to do," the Dr. asked." You just dropped a bomb on me. No I don't know what I want to do," I said. "Think it over; you'll be a great mom Brooke," the doctor said and walked out of the room.

Holy fuck, I'm pregnant, a baby? I'm so messed up I never even gave that a thought. What is Jonathon going to say? What are my parents going to say? What am I going to do? My brain feels like a hamster on a wheel, going round and round and the thoughts and images keep coming. I have to get out of here and call Sarah; she'll know what I should do. Better yet, I'm going to her house. I did about 90mph to her house. I ran to the door and knocked and her mom let me in.

Oh no, what will she think of me, she's like a second mother to me.

Her mom told me that Sarah was up in her room, I ran up there and I was out of breath. I collapsed on her bed sobbing. Sara had no idea what was going on. "Brooke, what's wrong," she asked. "I am pregnant!" "Are you serious, do you know for sure," she asked. "Yes, I just left the doctor's office, what am I going to do?" "Did you tell Jon yet?" "No, I came straight here and he's at his new job." "If we leave now, we can get to his place by the time he gets out of work. You have to tell him Brooke." "I know. Will you really come with me Sarah?" "Of course I will, whatever you decide I'll support you no matter what."

"I'll drive though; you need to chill out." "That's fine with me; I don't think I could drive anyway." This ride feels like it's much longer than before. I'm terrified to see his reaction. Will he be happy? Will we get married? Thoughts like that make me happy. Will he hate me? Will he hurt me? I really have no idea of his reaction; he can sometimes be a Jeckle and Hide. We're getting closer to his place and I'm terrified. "Sarah, I'm scared," I cried. "What are you most scared of, Jonathon or having a baby? You love babies, Brooke; you always talk about how you can't wait to be a mom. "Yeah, I would have hoped to be married first Sarah. I hope he'll be happy, but I don't know and that's what scares me so much."

"Shit Sarah, he's home." Seeing his car as we pulled up to the house, I began to panic even more.

"It's going to be okay Brooke, take a deep breath and go on inside. I'll wait out here. Remember Brooke, you always tell me how much the two of you are in love, trust in it." I reached for the door handle to get out and smiled at Sarah, taking in a deep breath. As my feet hit the ground, I could feel my body starting to tremble. I got up to the door and knocked. He opened the door and was in shock to see me there, "Are you okay, what are you doing here?"

"Jonathon, we need to talk, is your roommate here?" "No, but he will be shortly." "Can we go to your room in case he comes home?" I walked ahead of him in the room and noticed all my pictures were gone. I didn't dare ask why, not now.

"Brooke, what is it, are you sick, what is it, you're making me really worried?" "Jonathon, I'm pregnant," I blurted out. "How, when, I thought you were on the pill? We were always very careful about you taking it on time." His voice was shaking along with his body. "I took my pills, I don't know how this happened either," I said sobbing. "The calendar brings me back to the last time we were under the Weeping Willow Tree. Remember that perfect night. I felt something different happen that night," I cried. His demeanor changed.

"So, what are you planning on doing about this situation," he scorned. "Situation? Are you fucking kidding me? This is a baby…our baby. I don't know, what am I supposed to do?" "You need to have an abortion, that's what you need to do," he said so cold. "You want me to kill our baby Jonathon? I love you Jonathon, I can't kill this baby," I cried. "There's no other choice Brooke, this is for your own good. I promise. You haven't finished school yet. I just started a job, and you can't have this baby! You're going to stay here with me and we're going to take care of this, do you hear me," he demanded.

"This is not a flat tire or a broken window Jonathon. We are talking about a fucking baby that you and I made out of love," I sobbed. "My mother told me you would try and trap me and I didn't believe her and now you have proven her right," he said. "Fuck you Jonathon! This isn't my fault! I took my pills," I yelled. "If you had, we wouldn't be talking about this!" "I did, you son of a bitch! I don't know what happened. My doctor said that the pill isn't 100%." "Have you told anyone yet," he asked. "Just Sarah, she's in the car." "Well, you go and tell her you're not leaving with her and she can go."

Feeling like a scared and broken child, I went out to the car and told her I was staying here for the weekend and we were going to talk about it. Sarah saw how upset I was and didn't want to leave. I told her it was all okay and I'll call her when I get home. I gave her a hug and thanked her for driving me and she left. I went back in the house and Jon was throwing things around the house. "Stop it Jonathon, please. This is hard enough without your temper," I cried.

He reached for a phone book and started flipping through for a clinic to take me to. "Is it that easy for you, Jonathon to kill something we created? I thought you loved me? I thought you wanted me to be yours. Was that all a lie Jonathon, was it, tell me you asshole," I said now sobbing. "Brooke, you would never understand, of course I love you, I always have and I always will but we cannot have a baby, trust me on this, please."

"So this is it, I'm going to have a part of me ripped

out of my body and things will go back to normal? Say
something Jonathon," I begged. He just sat there and
cried out, "why did this happen? Why now? Why am I
being punished?" "What are you talking about
Jonathon? We are in love. We made love and this baby
is out of love. How is that a punishment? Answer me
goddamn it, you owe me that much," I shouted. "I
can't right now, the clinic is open until 8:00 we need
to go." "Just like that? Do I have a choice?" "No, it's
for your own good Brooke, please trust me on this,
please, we have to go before it's too late."

We had to walk through picket lines to get to the
clinic. The anti-abortion protestors were out in full
force, screaming at me "Baby killer, Murderer" as we
walked to the door. Jonathon was holding me up and I
was shaking beyond my control. A nurse came over to
us and took us into a room where they had me take my
pants off and gave me a gown. The room was stark
white, no pictures on the walls and it smelled of death.
"I can't do this Jonathon, don't make me, this is our
baby and we love each other," I cried. "There's no
other choice, if you don't do this, it will be worse for
you, I promise." Nothing is making sense to me. What
the fuck is he talking about?

The doctor came with consent forms to sign. I had a
hard time putting the pen to paper, but the look in
Jon's eyes made me sign. She put my legs in the
stirrups and turned on this machine. I saw a movie on
this once when a girl was raped. I wasn't raped, this is
so wrong, it has to stop, I yelled to the doctor. "Stop,
please stop!" I pleaded with her but it was too late.
"I'm sorry Brooke, we're finished," she said. Just like
that, a mere five seconds you just killed my baby, I
cried. I looked to Jonathon and he was crying and

couldn't look at me.

"Brooke, take a minute and collect yourself and I'll meet you at the counter in front," said the killer doctor. "Jonathon, I'll never forgive you for this! Never," I said. "Brooke, I'm so sorry and someday, believe me, you'll know it was for the right reasons," he said. "C'mon let's get out of here, you need to lie down," he said compassionately. We went out to the counter and the dr. had after care instructions for me. She was so kind to tell me I could be a little crampy and to wear a pad because of the bleeding. We walked out the back door where the protestors were not.

It was so impersonal, so cold and humiliating. It was no big deal for the doctor. She just killed an innocent baby; I'll never forgive Jonathon or myself. Jonathon and I got in the car, he grabbed my hand, and I pulled it back. He didn't push it; he pulled into the store and got me some pads and a box of Kudos. "Jonathon, the Kudos are sweet but they're a lie. Furthermore, you aren't mine anymore; you proved that to me, making me kill our baby." "Brooke, please believe me, someday you'll understand. I love you more now than ever." "What are you talking about Jonathon," asking, getting more upset by the second. He didn't reply. His head hung low and his color was on the greenish side.

We went inside and he carried me up the stairs, put me in his bed, and got me some orange juice. He was being kind, but why now? Looking around the room and all of the pictures of me are gone, why and where did they go? "Jonathon, where are my pictures?" At that instance, from the angle I was at, I saw them on the side of his dresser, shattered. "Why are our pictures all broken on the floor over there Jonathon?

Why?

"Brooke, there's some things I need to tell you. Please just let me speak and then you can respond. When I met you, I wasn't looking for anything more than a good fuck. I never planned to fall in love. By the time we got up to my room that first night, I already knew that I was in trouble with you. I felt something for you instantly. That first night you told me you loved me, I wanted to say it back, but I was terrified if I did, you would hurt me and I couldn't do that again. The night I got the hog award, it was awful, she was disgusting and I threw up after. It was then; I knew I loved you for sure. Then there was when I heard you were making out with Jeff, I thought I'd lose my mind. I was in a rage at the thought of you being with another guy. Someone tasting your sweet lips and touching your body, hearing your sweet moans of pleasure, it made me crazy. I never meant to hurt you that night and I'm so very sorry," he continued.

"When we made love under the Weeping Willow Tree that last time, I too felt something so beautiful and powerful. You have never been anything less than perfect to me and sometimes, it's scared me because I feared losing you. Just being with you, doing nothing, made me happy and whole. When I'm around you though, I want to be as close to you as possible. Brooke, you taught me more than I could ever teach you. Please never look back and doubt my love for you, promise me that. Know this too, you were my first true love and you'll always own that. You've had my heart from day one and you will until the end of time," he said with tears now falling.

"Jonathon why are you telling me this? Why are you crying, what is it," I asked confused? "Brooke, there's more. This is so hard for me to tell you." "Stop stalling and tell me because I am getting scared." He took a deep breath and began.

"The company I'm working for is Steph's dad's company." "WHAT," I shouted. "Her parents were divorced when she was young and he moved to Connecticut and opened this huge Engineering Firm, it's one of the best in the country." "Okay, so what does this mean, Jonathon," I asked. "I'm being blackmailed."

"Her father hired me and told me within 2 years, when he retired, the company would be mine if I was with Steph. Please don't say a word, let me explain, he said. I just have to be with her for two years and then we can be together, it will mean nothing to me." "Are you out of your fucking mind Jonathon?"

"I know how this sounds, and I'm sorry. I didn't have money when I was growing up and this is an opportunity for me to make it big. Please know that I fought this and I refused it at first, but Steph threatened to kill you and I know she's serious. She is crazy Brooke and I couldn't live if something happened to you."

"Jonathon, I might as well be dead, you just made me kill our baby and you just killed me so you did the work for her, take me home," I cried. "No, please, she's already tried to kill you. When you were here last time, Jamie caught her screwing with the breaks in your car. I can't risk her killing you. This is a sacrifice for me too, I want to be with you, but it's too risky, Steph knows I love you, she knows I want to spend the rest of my life with you. She's crazy like the woman from the movie we saw. Brooke, this all to save your life, I love you that much to give you up."

"So, let me guess, the phone calls weren't telemarketers, they were her?" "Yes, they were. She has been threatening me for a while of her plans." "Is she the girl that gave you the best blow job ever under the bleachers in High School," I asked. "Brooke, please don't, you don't want to know the answer."

"Have you been with her since you've been here," I asked not really wanting to know the answer. "She's been here, not by invitation, she came looking for you. She was drinking and she was on a rampage." "Did you fuck her Jonathan?" "No, she tried but I said no, that's when she threw all the pictures." "Fuck her, your mother must be thrilled with this arrangement, didn't you tell me she loved Steph. This was your plan was all along, wasn't it? You got me to fall in love with you, to make yourself feel better about yourself. You knew all along you were going to work for this guy!" "No! I swear it wasn't like that Brooke." "Well Jon, Steph told me she would win in the end and she was right. You two deserve each other."

"I'm not driving home with you! I'll take a fucking bus or walk before I get in the car with you!" Getting out of the bed, I doubled over with cramps. "Are you okay Brooke?" "What I am is no longer your concern. Do you think you could at least call me a cab to get to the bus station?" "Brooke, it's only two years, can't you wait for me?" "Are you for real Jonathon, you want me to go home and suffer for the next two years while you're in bed with her so you can be rich, go fuck yourself. You told me you didn't deserve me, well, you were right. What we had Jonathon was one of a kind and now it's over! Don't call me, don't write, I never want to see you again! I really hope it's worth it for you. You just killed two people with one stone you son of a bitch," I cried.

He tried to grab me as I went outside to wait for a cab and I fell to the ground, hysterical, my whole life just passed before me. "Brooke, I'm sorry, I love you." "Don't you ever say those words to me again Jonathon Sears. Your love is empty and your wallet is open, I hate you," I yelled as the cab pulled up.

I want to die with my baby. I don't think I can get through this; the love of my life just killed me. I'll never trust again. He just proved to me what I always thought years ago. I am nothing; I'm dispensable and can be traded for money. I paid the cab driver and boarded the bus to home, which I'm not looking forward to the questions from my mom. No longer will I protect him.

Back at his house, Jonathon is a mess; he knows that he just gave up the best thing that ever happened to him...for money, nonetheless. He didn't want to end it but he had no choice. He had to save my life. He loved me that much, so he says. Completely unbelievable, it reminds me of the movie we saw. How blind and stupid and I?

Arriving at the bus station, I called my mom to

come pick me up. She had no idea I had even gone anywhere. She was confused at the very least. She drove up and I began to cry harder. "What the hell happened to you Brooke? Are you all-right, you look like you were just raped or something." "Mom, can we just get home and I'll tell you about it then?" "Yes, Honey."

Thankfully, my dad was out of town, yet again. He couldn't know about this, he would kill Jonathon. As much hate I have for him now, I don't wish him death. Mom came and sat down next to me and handed me a ginger ale. "Brooke, what happened to you?" "Mom, it's a long story and I'll try and explain.

When we were at school, it wasn't all good. Jonathon and I fell in love fast and I hadn't known much about him. Noelle had set us up. He immediately had power over me, his looks, and his laugh captured me from that first night. It was intense, we were intense," I started to explain.

"There was this girl Steph that lived in the dorm across the street from mine. She was evil. She slashed my tire, she intimidated me and she tried everything to break us up," I went on to say. "Why did she want you broken up?" "At the time, I only knew that they had slept together once or twice, but she was obsessed with Jon. She and Noelle plotted together. They set up this girl to be in bed with him when Noelle knew I was bringing him breakfast one morning," I continued on to say.

"Brooke, I'm so sorry about this, this is crazy." "Mom, it gets so much worse. Noelle made up a lie that when I came home that weekend, I slept with Josh. Of course, I didn't but she told Jon I did. He flipped out, he chased me to my car and while I was trying to speed away in reverse, he opened my door, I fell out, and the car ran me over. "He ran you over? Brooke, what kind of guy is this, she yelled. Defending him, I said, "I fell out of the car, it wasn't his fault."

"When we were together and out of that environment mom, it was magical. He was wonderful to me and he made me feel loved, needed and wanted. His mom hates me and let me know that Jon would miss the career of his dreams if he were with me. Jon told me he would take care of her and he did set his mom straight. At least in front of me anyway. When we came home from Maine, mom, there was a package for me. It was a framed photo of Jonathon and Steph together from years before. He explained to me that they had gone out in high school and he hadn't been with her since his freshman year, but she was stalking him."

"Jon had always talked about his dream of working for this Engineering Firm; it was one of the biggest in the country. Low and behold, he got the job and I was so happy and proud of him.

I haven't been feeling good for a while mom, nauseous and tired so I went to the doctors today. I was pregnant." "What do you mean, was," mom asked staring at me. "I'm so sorry mom, Sarah brought me to Connecticut to tell Jonathon and that didn't go so well."

"He told me I had no choice but to have an abortion. He said it was for my own good. He brought me to a clinic mom it was horrifying. We had to walk through picketers and the room was reeking of death. I tried to stop it, but it was too late. He kept telling me mom that it was for me, it had to be done for me. It made no sense to me. Mom I loved him so much and I know he loved me, how could he do this to me," saying with a sob. Mom grabbed me and hugged me and she cried with me. "Mom, it gets worse." "I'm so sorry Brooke, what a son of a bitch!"

"He told me he was getting blackmailed." "By whom," mom asked. "The company he's working for is Steph's dad's company. Her dad told him the company would be his in two years if he was with his daughter." "He gave you up for money, that no good piece of shit," she slammed her hands. "He told me that Steph was going to kill me and that she had already tried by cutting the brakes in my car but his roommate caught her and stopped her. He told me we could be together in two years and I told him I hated him and to fuck himself. I had to get out of there so I took a bus home."

"Brooke, why didn't you tell me any of this while it was going on?" "Mom, I loved him so much and I really thought we would get married and I didn't want you to hate him." "Well, I hate him now! Brooke, maybe this Steph girl is dangerous and he really was trying to protect you, maybe he gave you up because he truly loved you."

"His mom has something to do with this, I know it and of course money. He said he didn't have a lot while growing up." "I think what you have to do Brooke is, keep the good memories and remember that you had what most people only dream of and you need to try to move on and forget about him. It wasn't meant to be Brooke and in a roundabout way, I think he did you a favor in the end."

"It hurts mom, it really hurts, I hate him and love him and he made me kill our baby." "I don't agree with what you did Brooke, but I think it was best in the end. What if you had the baby and that crazy girl did something to it, you would feel worse than you do right now."

Mom always made sense to me and she supported me no matter what. "Mom, I'm sorry I disappointed you, I'm so sorry." "You could never disappoint me Brooke, I'm sorry I wasn't there for you all those times." I couldn't talk anymore; I'm completely drained from rehashing it all. I got off the couch, I had to go to bed, I turned to mom, "I'm going to bed now, thank you mom and I love you so much," I gave her a hug and went to bed.

The next few weeks were not without conflict. Jonathon kept calling and I wouldn't talk to him. He sent me a letter:

Dear Brooke:

I miss you. Please read this letter, don't throw it away. I'm dying without you; I can't sleep, eat or do my work. I hate what I did to you and I hate Steph so much. I would rather be poor and with you than rich and without you. I still love you, will you ever forgive me? You were the perfect one for me, you got me, and you accepted me for who and what I was.

Brooke, I wanted our baby, but I couldn't let you have it, she would have killed you and the baby. I could not live myself knowing she would do that. Sometimes I wish I never met you so you would not have to hurt, but then I think how happy we were together and how you made me feel and I would not trade it for the world.

I love you and I miss you,

Kudos, Jonathon

Another couple of weeks passed and I decided to write him a letter back. I swore I wouldn't but for me, it was part of the healing process.

Dear Jonathon:

Please don't write me anymore. You and I are over! You made your choice, remember; it is all about choices. You have to live with your choices now and I'm sorry for you that you chose money over love.

You taught me another thing; never to trust anyone. You were the best manipulator and you were cunning in the process, you have more skills than you did in bed that I never knew about. Jonathon, this is your loss, not mine and I'm glad that I found out now, so I can go on with my life and find the man that truly wants me and not money. You took something that I thought was beautiful and tarnished it by greed and for that I will never forgive you. I sincerely hope that you and Steph are happy together and you become that rich man you so desire to be. I am no longer yours, so please leave me alone.

Brooke

The next few weeks, I didn't hear from Jonathon, he must have gotten the hint. My classes have started and I've met some nice people. It's a challenging course load, but it's what I need right now. I've set up an office in Rob's old room; just being in his room makes me feel like I'll come out of this with strength and dignity. He always made me feel better about myself, but Jonathon snowed him. I wasn't the only one, which made me feel a bit less blinded.

Through the next several months, I focused on school and friendships and wasn't ready for the dating scene yet. My friend Mandy from school tried to set me up on a few occasions, but I refused. The simple thought of being with a man was frightening to me. Unfortunately, I no longer felt I could trust and my self-esteem was yet again shattered.

I was lonely, there was no mistaking that and I did miss Jonathon. Often times achingly so, but there were good moments and bad as with everything. My head tried to convince me to forget him, but my heart was fighting it. After 6 months of not seeing him, I was missing him more and it was a sickness to me. He was toxic to me, the thoughts of us making love, then to the lies, it wasn't healthy and I had to move on.

The only way I felt I could move on was to re-enter the world, finally. The only way I could do that was to say good-bye to the past. On this day, I got his fraternity coat, the pin he so fucking nicely gave to me, the pearl ring, the stuffed animal, everything went into a box except for one thing, I couldn't part with his Navy T-shirt. I folded a small note inside the box for him that read:

Jonathon,

Material things are nothing; it's what is in your heart that is everything. These items mean nothing to me anymore because you showed me your true heart,

which I think, is empty. Brooke

I sent it off by Fed Ex and I finally felt freer than I had in months.

A part of me feels free and alive; another part of me feels afraid of this freedom as well. It's time for me to get my head clear and be free. Decision made, I'm heading to the Mountains for the weekend alone. While driving the 3-hour drive, I found myself fantasizing about a man's touch. A one night stand even. I'm getting tingly just thinking about it. Arriving at the Inn, it's cozy and very rustic, the smell of the winter air and crackling wood makes me think of intimacy, and I want it. When I got into my room, there was a double bed with a purple satin spread; there was a desk and a reclining chair in the corner of the room. Next to the bed there was an ice bucket chilling a bottle of wine that had been awaiting my arrival.

Noticing a Hotel Guide of Services, I saw they had a spa. This was the time for me; I deserve to pamper myself. I called the spa and booked a massage, a haircut, wax and pedicure. The massage was the first appointment. How I needed to unwind and be relaxed.

Sitting in the waiting area for the therapist to call me in, I began to think yet again about my wants. Then I heard my name called. In front of me stood a tall, 6-foot man with black hair and blue eyes and teeth that were big and bright. A man, I said to myself, I've never had a man massage therapist. I hesitated for a moment then said to myself, you're free and this is your new start. I followed him to the massage room. The room had little to no light. Soft music was playing in the background and the smells of aromatherapy. It was peaceful. David was his name. He told me to remove my clothing, and he'd be back in a moment. All of my clothing, I'm asking myself; he didn't say to leave anything on so, all it is.

He came back and I was lying face down on the heated table. "Do you have any trouble areas you want me to focus on," he asked. "The whole body, including my heart," I replied. He began with my head, rubbing my temples and moving down to my face and neck. His hands were strong and soft at the same time. I found myself aroused by his touch. He moved his hands down to my thighs and I was getting wet, fantasizing about him getting on top of me. What is the matter with me? I don't even know him, but his touch feels so warm and comforting.

He had me turn over and he moved the sheet down to massage my stomach and my breasts are exposed. I was oddly comfortable with this. He was gentle and he never said a word. He moved down to the front of my thighs and I started to tingle in that region. He moved on to my feet and I let out a moan. He said, "Brooke, you like this, don't you?" I mumbled. "Yes." The sultry voice he had and the, "You Like this don't you," reminded me of Jonathon. My body is a mass of sensations. He'd finished and left me to get clothed. I sat in the chair drinking water and my whole body was sizzling with desire.

David returned after I was dressed and told me to drink plenty of water for the rest of the day. Dehydration can happen after a massage. I stared at him, he staring back; I was throbbing between my legs. I got up, said thank you, and went to have my haircut.

Walking into the hair salon, there were gay men everywhere, and there were no women. It was awesome. I told them my name and James welcomed me. He got me a cup of tea and brought me to his station. He asked me, "Beautiful, what would you like done today?" "James, I want to look sexy and free," I smiled. He said, "Oooh, I love it, I'll get started right now." He swiveled the chair away from the mirror and said, "Girl, I'm going to make you look like fire. You are going to be smoking when you leave here." I smiled back at him. Taking in his facial expressions and hand gestures, it was awesome.

Excitement hit my stomach and I was ready for this change. James was snipping away and I could see that my long hair wasn't going to be so long anymore. James was full of expression and passion about his work. After cutting and cutting, he put my head into a cap and began pulling my hair through it. He was coloring my hair, which I'd never had done before. I had no idea what color and frankly, I didn't care.

After he was finished with pulling my hair through the cap, he put me under the dryer for 20 minutes. Even his touch was turning me on, a gay man's touch. I couldn't help but think about Dave, the Massage guy. He was so sexy, and I didn't see a wedding ring on his finger either as I think of it. A stranger, I'm yearning for him. So bizarre for me.

The timer went off and James came back and brought me to the sink to shampoo. He was so gentle and the hot water running over my head, it was making me hornier. He brought me back to his station, blew dry my hair and turned me to the mirror. "I'm a blonde now," I said. "You want to be sexy, and this Brooke, is sexy," he said. My hair is short now with a bounce and sass to it and I love it.

I went over, had my eyebrows waxed, and that wasn't as relaxing as the previous services. Onto to the pedicure, love having my feet rubbed. An American man, not Chinese. He massaged my feet and my toes and up to my mid- calf. Then he clipped my toenails and polished them in a deep red. He painted a daisy on the first and last toe of each foot. This also turned me on, wet hands rubbing my feet.

After I was finished with my makeover, so to speak, I went up to my room. I went in my suitcase and got my red bikini on. When looked in the mirror, I felt sexy and beautiful. Renewed and ready for anything. I went down to the hot tub. When I got in the spa area, there was a couple in the hot tub. They were making out. I just sat, and stared, they hadn't noticed I was there. They obviously thought they were alone. They were fondling each other and I almost started playing with myself, it turned me on. The woman turned and saw me and got out of the hot tub embarrassed. The man followed her and they left. It was now my turn with the hot bubbles.

I got in, rested my head on the side, and nearly fell asleep. My mind kept thinking of David from the massage. I had to see him again. I wanted him. His hands were magical on my body and I wanted more of that…. from him. I couldn't stop thinking of him and I couldn't control myself any longer. I put my hands down my bathing suit bottoms and began to rub myself. Thinking of him next to me in the hot tub and what I wanted him to do to me, I climaxed. On my own, this was a first for me.

I left the spa room and went back to my room to get dressed and go to the bar. Taking off my bathing suit and laying out my clothes for the night, I stood in front of the mirror and looked at my nakedness. I want him is all I was thinking of, I want him in me, on me, all over me. I can dream, and this dream is making me wet again. I put on my tight, short red skirt and a black button down shirt and black high-heeled boots, James was right, I was smoking.

I took a seat at the bar and ordered myself a Cosmopolitan. The bar wasn't crowded, they had a pianist playing, and it reminded me of my dad. I didn't want to think of him though; I wanted to think of David. After another Cosmo, I heard a vaguely familiar voice speaking to the bartender. Was that his voice? I don't know anyone here; it has to be. "I'll have a captain and coke please," he said in his deep tone.

It was David. He sat down next to me and he didn't recognize me at first. Since I saw him this morning, I had had a haircut and a color from brown to a blonde-haired woman. My body is screaming for him and I don't even know him. I said, "Hello," and he said, "hello," still not sure if he recognized me. "David?" "Yes… Brooke, right, from this morning, you look stunning, and you changed your hair." "Yes, I had the full makeover today." "You didn't need one, but it's not hard on the eyes, I'll tell you. You look fantastic."

I blushed for a moment and my crotch began to

throb. He had a white button down shirt on with jeans. I could see his bulge through his pants and I couldn't help but stare. He bought me a drink and I then put my hand on his thigh. He didn't move it; he grabbed it and moved it to his inner thigh. I could feel him getting aroused. I smiled at him and he back. He untucked his shirt to hide what was growing underneath and I stood up. I took a step and looked back at him; I caught his stare and motioned him to follow. He got up, carefully and followed me to the elevator. There were no words. The elevator door opened and we entered, pressed third floor. I have high heels on and I'm still so much shorter than he is. He picked me up, and put his mouth over mine. He kissed me ferociously; his tongue was down my throat.

The elevator stopped and we walked to my room, in silence. I opened the door and I let him in before me. I pushed him down on the Satin bedspread. My eyes never leaving his, I unzipped his pants, and he was hard. I pulled his pants down and I began to rub his cock, it was perfect, the area was shaven and it was smooth. I put him in my mouth; he took my clothes off and turned me around in the 69 position. He opened my lips and slipped his tongue inside me. I'm going deeper on him as he is licking me, barely being able to breathe.

He added a finger to his tongue. He massaged my clit, and I couldn't hold on anymore, he said, "Stop sucking. I want to feel your insides with my cock." He made me come. I got on top of him and rode him hard, back and forth, and he grabbed my back, pulled me closer to him, and stared in to my eyes. He kissed my lips with pressure and he came.

Without many words said, this was incredible. He

got up and got the bottle of wine that is now in melted ice and we both drank from the bottle. He then began to massage my feet and he spoke, "I remember you loved this, this morning. Your body is so soft Brooke. I thought of you all day. I thought of how I wanted to taste you, I knew you would taste so sweet."

I got up, went into the bathroom, and started the shower. I got in and he joined me. He pushed me up against the wall and fucked me so hard, all I could say was, "Don't stop, and fuck me harder", and he did. I leaned over the tub and he entered from behind, cupping my breasts and thrusting so I could feel him deep in me. He then turned me around, licked my lips, sucked my ear, and then licked the water off my face. I grabbed his ass and brought him deeper in me, "more", I said, "More" and he came.

We got out of the shower, thirsty, we both guzzled from the bottle of wine. Not many words were spoken. I handed him his clothes and said, "It's getting late and I need to get some sleep." His tall body standing in front of me, looking down at me, he whispered, "I will never forget this night." "Neither will I, thank you."

Freedom is delicious I thought to myself. Very unlike me but it was hot, sexy, and satisfying. I went to sleep with the memories of sex with a stranger. Oh how good it felt, no strings, not nothing but pure delicious attraction.

I woke up, went and had breakfast in the lounge area downstairs. While eating breakfast, I could still feel the impact in my crotch area from his pulsating cock slamming into me. Smiling, I went to check out and start the three-hour drive home, feeling as free as a butterfly.

Glancing at myself in the rearview mirror, I wasn't ashamed. I felt desirable and wanted and this is what I needed, this weekend proved to me that I'm in control for the first time in a long time. I'm in control of me. No strings attached, no ownership, just good raw sex. If I'm in control and have no expectations, I can't get hurt. I'm now in protective mode.

Getting home was nice, but reality of school kicked in. I had a big decision to make, am I going to change my major? I'm thinking of changing to Psychology. It seems a better course for me so I can help people. I don't want anyone to go through what I did with Jonathon. I'm meeting with my advisor on Monday.

A cup of tea and a piece of toast in hand, heading to the school, I'm ready to make my decision about my major. I walked into the Advisor's office with a navy blue suit on and brief case in my hand. I asked Shirley, the advisor, "How many credits will transfer, will this change my graduating time?" "All of your credits will transfer and your graduation date will not be affected," Shirley said. Therefore, it's finished; I'm now a Psychology major. I'm excited about it and ready to switch to those classes. It's going to be challenging, but I don't think any more than law. Everything that I knew about myself when I was with Jonathon is changing. It has to be this way.

Thoughts of him simmer; I wonder if he's with Steph? Is he happy? Does he think of me? What would he think of me fucking a stranger? I need a psychologist for myself. I still love him. Why can't I forget him? I have to stop thinking about him. My stomach is in knots and I suddenly feel guilty for having a one-night stand. I'm making myself crazy.

After classes, I went home, ate dinner, and studied. Mandy called for me to go out, but I declined. She had no idea what I had done over the weekend. I told her and she was surprised and proud of me. However, I needed a break now. Snuggled up in my pajamas and I started to write in my journal.

Monday:

This weekend I had the most amazing time. I got a massage, a haircut and a pedicure that was fantastic. James was awesome. I became someone I never knew existed inside of me. I had hot, dirty sex without words and it was unbelievable. This guy was hot and he wanted me as much as I wanted him. I was in control and I am not his, I am mine and only mine and it feels good. I don't know why I'm still thinking of Jonathon, Fuck. I wish him well, goodnight.

The next few weeks were crazy busy with school and papers that had to be written. It was good to be living at home because I didn't have to waste time at the Laundromat or be around all the drama that dorm life supplied. I'm happy with my decision to transfer and change my major.

Finally, Mandy got me to go out with her. We went to a bar where they had a band and we danced and drank shots. She was seeing a guy Tom, he was there, and he had a friend. Ben. Ben was built like a rock; he was cute, not gorgeous, but very appealing. He had thin lips, brown hair and brown eyes; he was going for his doctorate in computer engineering.

Mandy left him and I, while her and Tom went to dance, we chatted and drank more. He was a nice guy. We all ended up leaving together and Mandy and I couldn't drive so Ben brought us home. He dropped them off first and then went on to bring me home. We got to my driveway and it was 1 am. He asked, "Can I kiss you?" I was surprised that he asked and I leaned toward him and whispered," I'd like that." His kiss was nice and he had a little bite with it, which was different but sexy and nice. We sat in the driveway kissing and talking until 5 am. He never tried anything else on me. He was a nice guy and I liked him.

I went inside at 5am and got into bed and thought, I could see myself with him, he's kind and a gentleman. Not sure if he'll call me, but I hope he does. The next day after class, I had a message from Ben asking me if I would like to go to his lake house with him on the weekend. I got butterflies; I hadn't felt that in a long time. I returned his call and said yes. Mandy and Tom were going too.

After class, I packed my things and got ready to head to Maine with Ben, Mandy and Tom. I was a little nervous to stay the weekend with Ben, but he was so nice, it helped. We drove 4 hours and I slept at least half the way in the back seat with Mandy. We stopped at the grocery store when we got in town and got some beer and some food to cook for dinner.

We pulled into the dirt road of Ben's family place; it was right on the water. It was cottage like, but bigger, two bedrooms a kitchen and a living room and a screened porch looking out at the lake. It was nice, but smelled a bit musty; it doesn't get a lot of use, so it's closed up often. I put my things in the room with Mandy and she said, "No, Tom is in here with me, you're with Ben," I felt panicky. I brought my things and set them down in the living room for now.

I told them I would make spaghetti for dinner and while that was cooking, we played drinking games. We laughed and had a great time. It being winter, we couldn't really do much in the way of lake activities. We lit a fire outside and sat around it after dinner, telling scary stories and being silly. Mandy and Tom went in to go to bed and Ben and I stayed out by the fire and talked.

We talked about everything and he asked me about Jonathon. Mandy had told him about our breakup. It was a bit uncomfortable talking about it with another guy, but he listened and he shared about his previous girlfriend. He held my hand and rubbed my palm with his fingers. It was nice. We went inside and he said, "You can have the bedroom, I'll sleep in the living room on the couch." I felt bad, it was his place, after all, so I said… "And we can both stay in the bedroom, if you want." I got changed into sweatpants and a t-shirt and he was in his boxers. He had an amazing body. His chest was solid and he had a six-pack with hair running down his trail. He was sexy. I got into bed and we talked some more and he grabbed my face and kissed me softly. There was something very different about him; he was just a very kind man. He did nothing but kiss me and we fell asleep in each other's arms.

We woke up in the morning and we went out to breakfast and of course Mandy was wondering if I had sex with him. She and I went to the ladies' room and she asked," So did you have sex with him?" "No, we didn't but we had an amazing night and he's such a great guy." "Yes he is that's why I think he's perfect for you and you deserve a guy like him Brooke." We both smiled and went back to the table.

We had a great weekend, we played games and ate lots of food and had no sex. I think I really like Ben. He's extremely smart, sexy, kind and gentle. I don't know where this will go, but I'm taking things slow this time.

Ben and I have been spending lots of time together on the weekends at his apartment at school. We haven't had sex yet, but I think we're both burning with desire. I feel I may be ready very soon. When I'm with him, I feel pampered and respected. This weekend we're going to a wine tasting; just the two of us and back to his apartment.

He was wearing jeans, a turtleneck and a black sweater and cowboy boots, and he looked so sexy. Something about the turtlenecks, I guess. His boots were something I hadn't expected him to be wearing. When he was at school in Texas, he bought them.

I, in a pair of black slacks and a red cowl neck sweater and my heeled black boots, we were ready to go for some tasting. He opened the car door for me, took my hand, and kissed it softly; tingles went all through my body. I care about him and I want to see all of him, feel all of him. I have no doubt he will be gentle and loving.

We walked in to the large ballroom where the vendors were set up for the tasting, hand in hand. I know nothing about wine, so he led the way. He asked, "Do you like sweet or dry wine?" "Sweet and wet," I said with a flirty smile. The first up was a Merlot, it was good, but dry, I said, "No, too dry, I like wet," flirting with him. There were Zinfandels, that were sweet and fruity and I liked that. We went to every table and drank wine and I was feeling very tipsy. There was a chocolate fountain set up in the middle of the ballroom with fruits that you could dip in. We pleasured ourselves with bananas and chocolate, strawberries and he even fed me a few; he was teasing me, as I was he.

"Ben, we have to get out of here, I can't take this anymore." He smiled and grabbed my hand and walked me to the car. While he was driving, his bulge was right there for me to examine. I wanted to see it, feel it, and taste it. What lies under his pants was still a mystery to me, but I need to unravel it.

We entered his apartment, it was dark, quiet and we were all alone. His roommate was away for the night, which left him and me and the effects of the wine. He turned on the kitchen light, went and grabbed something from the cabinet. He picked me up with his strong arms and placed me on the bed. He removed his turtleneck and sweater and waited to meet my eyes for approval to go further. He pulled his boots off, and then his pants and I watched him intently. He then reached his arms out and lifted me to pull my pants off, staring into my eyes, without a distraction. He then pulled my sweater off and I lie there naked in front of him for the very first time.

He took my arms and pulled me up to the head of the bed, from behind; he grabbed a long piece of rope and began tying my hands to the headboard. Never losing sight of my gaze, he cut another piece of rope and tied each leg to the bedposts. I was now spread eagle. He finally spoke and said, "Brooke, I have wanted you since the first night we met and I'm going to savor this and make you feel how you should feel, loved and pampered." I said nothing. I then moved my eyes from his and stared at his hard, long penis. It wasn't too big or too small, and I began to feel a bit nervous about this. Being tied up, he was in control.

He made sure I was okay and the ropes were not too tight, and he began his journey. He positioned his body next to mine and ran his fingers through my hair and behind my ears; he gave sweet kisses down my neck. It was gentle and I was getting very excited. "I want this night to last forever. I love you Brooke and I want to show you what real love is." I lay silent.

He poured chocolate syrup on my breast. It was cold, he began licking it off me, taking his mouth over my nipples and biting them gently. It certainly got hotter. My lower half kept trying to move and he pushed it down, "in due time." With one hand on my right breast and twisting my nipple, the other with his tongue, I was feeling heat down below, throbbing and a delightful wetness-taking place.

He kissed my belly and followed my trail with his tongue, moaning and enjoying every minute of his seduction. "Can I go further down on you?" I was a bit uncomfortable, but I smiled and nodded to him. He lowered himself in between my legs and kissed me. He went in a circle with his tongue around my sensitive spot, slow and steady and he was making me crazy. I couldn't move and he had full control. I didn't like that part, but with him, it was different. He put his finger inside, "you are so wet Brooke," and I pulled my hips up to him and he added another finger. His tongue and fingers were swelling me up and it wasn't long before he brought me to orgasm.

He stopped and said; "I love you," again I fell silent. He untied my arms and legs and whispered, "I want to make love to you." He put his mouth to mine and inserted himself inside. He was so hard and long that he reached my G-spot. He held me tight as he moved himself further in me, then he came quickly. He pulled me on top of him, "I just want to hold you, to feel you on me."

We laid there for hours until we fell asleep, naked, satisfied with barely any words. In the morning, I awoke first and I found myself staring at him. This amazingly intelligent, sensitive, gentle man loved me, I thought to myself. I never said it back to him. Fear of those words and them being from me was hard for me to handle. He awoke and pulled me closer to him, "Brooke, last night was the best night of my life, you are beautiful, sexy and I love you. I know it is hard for you to say the words, but I could feel it with your body last night and it's okay."

We made love again and I could really feel his love. Weeks and months went by with us together on weekends and holidays and I did love him. It was a different kind of love but it was a safe love. He treated me so well and he was never afraid to tell me how he felt about me. I felt very lucky.

Eight months into our relationship, I was at home studying and the phone rang. I ran and answered it and I never expected to hear the voice on the other end. It was Jonathon. "Hello Brooke." "Hi." "Brooke, I need to see you." "Jonathon, I'm with someone else now. Seeing you wouldn't be fair to him. He loves me and I'm finally happy." "I love you Brooke." "Jonathon, if you loved me you would never have taken a job with strings attached." "I did it to save your life. Steph and I are over! I can't do it anymore. I'm getting a new job." "That's great Jonathon, but I'm finally happy again and I have a guy that respects me and loves me and treats me like a queen."

"Please, let me see you once; I miss you." He had a hold over me still. "Where would you like to have this meeting Jonathon?" "At the Weeping Willow Tree.," "You want me to go back there and relive everything we went through?" "I promise you, I will not touch you. I just need to see you, please." After going back and forth, I agreed to meet him on the weekend. "I know you still love me Brooke," I fell silent. "I'll meet you there at 12:00." He thanked me and at that moment, I had no idea what I was doing.

I couldn't tell Ben. I know it's wrong, but I have to do this for myself as well. I haven't been able to give myself to him completely for eight months and he deserves only the best. If I see Jonathon this one time, maybe I'll be able to love Ben the way he wants and so deserves.

It worked in my favor; Ben had to meet with some friends for the weekend, so I wasn't canceling on him. He said he would miss me and he couldn't wait to make it up to me when he got back. I wish he wasn't so goddamn nice to me. I don't deserve him, nor do I know how to handle such a stable relationship. It's nice, but I'm always waiting for him to lose it on me or something as my past has dictated.

Feeling guilty about driving to see Jonathon, I asked myself what I was doing? How can I trust that he's not with Amazon Steph? How will I react when I see him? I'm so anxious and unsure. While driving down the familiar roads of college, a rush of memories came back to me. The passion we had, the beauty he possessed, the hurt, the lies and the Weeping Willow Tree.

Thankfully, the warm weather had arrived so he didn't torture me in his turtleneck. I know he would wear it for he knows how I liked it. My heart is racing as I approach the Weeping Willow. I see him up ahead. Every part of my being falls weak with the view of him. Fourteen months later and he still had this intensity about him and over me. Was it love or lust, or both? He saw me stopped and now staring at him. He walked toward me. As fit and as beautiful as ever, he got in front of me and I couldn't believe he was standing in front of me. It was as if no time had passed and the feelings were just as strong. He gave me a big hug that lifted my feet from the ground. He led me under the Weeping Willow Tree and I sat down on the ground and he beside me, it was surreal.

"You've changed Brooke. I can see it in your eyes. Your hair is different and you finally gained a bit of weight. Brooke, you are stunning." "Jonathon, why did you want to see me?" "Brooke, since you left that day on the bus, I have become a very bad person. I'm angry all the time and I ache without you." "Jon, you have Steph to get you through those tough times." "I hate her, she makes me sick, she isn't you babe." "Jon, don't call me that. You had me. I was yours and you gave it up and I had to move on."

He grabbed me and kissed me; just his lips sent me

reeling. "You still feel it Brooke, don't you?" "Jon, I have someone else and he loves me. He doesn't lie to me or cheat on me. "Do you love him?" "I should and a part of me does. He's an incredible guy who would never hurt me and he's put up with a lot of shit because of you." "What did I do? You left me Jon, you killed my heart and soul and poor Ben has had to suffer with my insecurities that you tattooed on me." "Does he touch you like I did?" "Jonathon, he touches me with grace and kindness, not desperation." "So, you fuck him?" "I wouldn't say we fuck, no, we make love and he loves me Jonathon." "Do you love him Brooke, one last time?" "I'm not sure I can ever love again after you. I loved you more than I loved myself, but it wasn't a healthy love for me."

"How can you say that our love wasn't healthy Brooke? Look at where we are, under the Willow Tree. Don't you remember the times we shared under here?" "Yes," with a tear coming down my face, "Jonathon, I could never forget. This is where our baby was made. This is where I first told you I loved you, and I'll never forget this place." "Please be mine again, Brooke."

"Jonathon, no, are you kidding me? I can never give anyone control over me again. You controlled me Jonathon; every part of me. My body, my whereabouts, my thinking, everything and I can't go back to that," I said, starting to cry. "Brooke, I need you. I love and miss you so much," he pleaded with me. "I'm sorry Jonathon; you sacrificed our love for money and sex with a fucking bitch who was threatening to take my life. How do you think that made me feel?"

Suddenly, he was on top of me and his mouth was

covering mine so I couldn't say a word. I was trying to wiggle my way from beneath him, but he wrapped his arms around me so tight. Tears are pouring down my face, as he is deep in my mouth with his tongue. I could feel him getting hard up against me. I tried to stop him, but he had power over me, but I wanted it to stop. I couldn't fight it or him any longer. He was rough and raw with me. He fucked me so hard, reminiscent of those desperate nights. This time was different, he was hurting me and I wanted him to stop, but he wouldn't. He exploded inside of me and left me lying there limp, unable to move.

He got up and said, "I needed that before my wedding." "What? You had me come here to fuck you, tell me you loved me and you're getting fucking married!" I screamed. "Yes, I know everything you've been doing. You fucked some guy in a hotel and you didn't even know him. You've been playing house with this Ben guy for way too long. I wanted to fuck you hard and hurt you like you have been hurting me for the last year and a half."

"I will always have control over you Brooke. You fucked me under this tree and your wonderful boyfriend knows about you coming here. Brooke, by the way, your relationship is over with him, you're used goods." "How can you be so cruel?" "I told you Brooke, I've been angry and not a good man and it's your entire fault. Everything is your fault; if you didn't walk into my fraternity that night, if you didn't spread your legs for that guy in the hotel; you have driven me to marry Steph, you and only you!" he said with a crazed look in his eyes.

I got up, and looked in his face and said, "You are fucking crazy Jonathon! Stay out of my life and don't think you can control me anymore, because you can't." "You better not fuck anyone else Brooke," he warned me.

"You are getting married Jonathon, I'm not yours anymore. I can do whatever I want!" He then grabbed my neck and squeezed it until I couldn't breathe. I released from him and ran. I was running so fast and I ran right into Steph, she was with him. It was all part of a plan.

I got to the edge of the park, I was nearing my car and I heard, "Brooke, why did you do it?" It wasn't Jonathon it was Ben. I turned to him and fell to the ground sobbing with no words to say that would make any difference. "I'm so sorry Ben, I'm so sorry. I never meant to hurt you," I cried. "I loved you Brooke and I was willing to wait for you to love me," he said. "I never thought you would fuck him," he said. "I tried to stop him Ben, I did, I am so sorry." "We are over Brooke and just so you know, you broke my heart." "Ben, wait! I was so wrong and I want you to know, you made me happy." "Not happy enough for you to lie about your plans and come down and fuck him under a Willow Tree," he snapped. "I had to find out if I still loved him. I never planned to fuck him. He fucked me. I couldn't move, it was not out of love, he fucked me. I told him to stop," I sobbed.

Steph and Jonathon sat and watched me try to get out of this mess. They were laughing but Jonathon didn't look happy. My whole world has turned upside down…. again. This time I was the wrongdoer; I never planned on this happening. I got into my car, my body and mind numb, my crotch throbbing in pain and my heart shattered. I looked out my window and saw Jonathon bending over with his hands covering his face, as if he was crying. Ben was kicking a tree and we were all hurting. How did this happen? Why can't they just leave me alone? Poor Ben, I feel awful.

Ben and I have been over for 5 months; he hasn't answered my calls or letters. He was a great guy and I broke his heart. Its amazing how one person can mess up your entire life? It's time for a change and I need to get out of here. Perhaps I'm only allowed to be happy for short periods. A teaser.

I called my friend Howard that had moved to Myrtle Beach and asked if I could stay with him for a while. I needed a thoughtless job and a clean break from it all. He said, "sure come on down." He and I always had a great time together. We laughed all the time. He did warn me, however, that he had a roommate. He was an older guy and he was very crotchety. I didn't care, anything was better than being here within a 2-hour distance from Jonathon and his fiancé.

I drove the 18-hour drive to Myrtle Beach and did lots of thinking on the drive. I was humiliated with myself. I felt like I was kicked in the gut. It all started over again 5 months ago, this time, it was pure evil. I needed a friend, someone who accepted me for who I was and could make me laugh at the drop of a hat.

Howard greeted me in the driveway, his smile

always made me smile. "Hey, you made it! Come on in. I'll show you your room, it's tiny." It was a nice condominium with two floors, a kitchen, dining area, living room and three bedrooms. It was on a golf course and the back porch looked out over the 15th hole. "This is beautiful, Howard. Thank you so much for letting me stay for a bit, it won't be long. I'm planning on waitressing for a while and finding my own place perhaps." "Hey, we needed a girl around here; we eat like shit, now you can cook for us."

We went out grocery shopping after I put my things away and we couldn't stop laughing. He was making fun of people in the store. I hated to laugh but he was hysterical. It felt good to be with a friend, someone I could trust. Nothing intimate, just two friends, this and us is what I need.

I cooked dinner for him and Ed. Filet Mignon with a Mushroom Gravy, twice-baked potatoes and fresh asparagus. We ate out on the porch as we watched the golfers down below. It was peaceful and quiet and I felt very much at ease. Later that night, I told Howard what had happened under the Weeping Willow Tree and he couldn't believe it. "I was glad when you and Jonathon broke up," he admitted. We talked and laughed for hours and I went in to bed in my new tiny room and slept like a baby.

In the morning, I went to a few restaurants and filled out applications for a server position. Then I went to the beach while Howard was at work and got some rays. It dawned on me how Jonathon knew about everything that I had done back home. It was Noelle, she'd been asking friends of ours and she talked with Jonathon and told him everything. She gave him Ben's phone number as well. That fucking bitch slut, I thought. It all made sense and it made me furious. I don't even talk with her anymore but she has some axe to grind with me. Well, she can't get me here. Realizing that, I lay back and shut my eyes.

Back from the beach, I was cooking dinner in my bathing suit when Howard and Ed came home from work. Ed, a dirty old man, said, "This is a nice thing to see when we come home, maybe next time you could be naked." "You're a pig Ed," I said and he chuckled. Howard and I got changed and we went and played some golf after we ate. I'm not very good at all but it was fun. "Brooke, it was sweet seeing you in your bathing suit when I got home. I had dirty thoughts about you after," he said. "Howard, you have dirty thoughts about everyone," I said and we laughed.

We had a great time golfing then we went back to the condominium. Howard had to work early in the morning and I had to look for work again. It had been a month since I had been there and still no word on a job. It's been amazing being out here, not trying to be perfect for anyone and just being me. Howard was a good man, not sure why he didn't have a girlfriend. He did have commitment issues though, so that may have something to do with it. When he was living in my hometown, he had a serious girlfriend and it had gone wrong, so maybe he's being cautious like me.

"Howard, I have to find a job. I saw a sign on the marquee at that Hotel on the beach. I'm going there tomorrow to apply." They had a formal dining room and they needed servers. I went in the morning and they hired me on the spot. The place was stunning, right on the ocean. I called Howard at work and told him. "Awesome! You and I are celebrating tonight!" "Sounds great Howard, see you soon."

I was getting ready in my room when Howard and Ed got home. I put on my red tank top, white shorts and black heels and went out to the kitchen where the boys were grabbing a beer. There was a bouquet of flowers in a green wrap set on the kitchen table. Howard brought them over to me and said, "Congratulations!" "Are you wearing underwear, Brooke," Ed asked. "Ed, you need to get laid," I chuckled. Howard went to change into some shorts and told me he's been dying to go to this bar and tonight they were having a lingerie show. "So Howard, you want me to sit and watch hot girls strut around in thongs and lingerie?" "Yes, or you could do it for me." I laughed and said, "I'm definitely going to need to get drunk." He laughed. We got to the bar and the runway was set up for the girls. The show hadn't started yet so we ordered a pitcher of beer and talked. He was comfortable to be around; we even played with each other's fingers on top of the table. He was my guy pal.

He ordered two Slow Comfortable Screw shots for us, Vodka, Kahlua and Baileys. ", Howard, you have one thing on your mind, this show better get started for you," I said laughing. We clanked our glasses and down the chute it went. He turned to me and said, "Why don't you join the show? You can do it. You are smoking." "No thanks. I could never do that and I'm not smoking. Just wait until they come out with their huge tits and tight asses, which isn't me."

The lights dim in the bar area and they shine on the runway. The first girl came out wearing tassels over her nipples and underwear that barely covered her vagina. Howard was bright red in the face; he had fair skin, so blushing was easy for him. I ordered the next pitcher; I warned Howard I would need a lot to get through this show. The girls came out, one after another with more or less on; I was getting a bit uncomfortable watching this with Howard as he was enjoying it all too much.

"Howard," I said with a slur, "How much longer are you going to torture yourself? I bet we don't leave this bar without you whacking off." "Well, you can do it for me Brooke." Both of us were very intoxicated. "Yeah, you wish Howard." "I sure do!" We left the bar and had to walk home as neither of us was sober enough to drive. We talked about the girls in the show and Howard shared his favorites. He was definitely a boob man, which kept me safe, I laughed to myself.

We both tiptoed inside the condominium not to wake up Big Ed; lord knows he would love to hear all about the lingerie show. I started walking up the stairs to my tiny bedroom and Howard walked behind me and asked, "So are you wearing underwear?" "Wouldn't you like to know?" I got one-step in my room and he pulled my shorts down. "Holy shit Brooke, you are wearing a thong that's better than no underwear."

"What are you doing Howard," I slapped his hand. "You know Brooke; you know we can't resist it anymore." "Howard, we're best friends and we're drunk." "C'mon, let me play with you Brooke." "We can have slow comfortable sex," he said and laughed. He grabbed my crotch and knelt down in front of me. "Howard, we can't," and he put his tongue on my pussy and I was now at his mercy. I'm up against the wall, my legs wrapped around his head and he's licking me with such skill. "Howard, you have to stop, I'm going to come, this isn't right." "Cum for me Brooke. I've waited a long time for this."

My best guy friend is making me come and I can't stop it. I don't want to stop it. I reached down and grabbed him, "Howard, your cock is Colossal." We both started laughing and suddenly, I had to have it. Now I know the beer and the shots are really kicking in. I put him in my mouth and it's hard to put my mouth around. Licking him up and down, he's getting harder and I can feel myself swelling down below. I can taste him getting close and I have to have this huge cock in me.

He pulled me down underneath him and he was now inside me with my juices making him slide in and out easily. He kissed my mouth and his kiss was nothing that I had expected, it was soft and sensual. He drove harder into me and the headboard was banging against the wall, then we slowed our pace to a "Slow and Comfortable Screw." He is so big that he hit every part of my insides and made me scream and wet him more. One hard thrust and he came. I could feel him pulsating and I was aching with satisfaction and soreness. Both of us started laughing and realized that this had been building up for a long time.

"Howard is your father an elephant," I asked laughing. "I've never seen anything that big and you maneuver it very well." "You weren't too shabby yourself; your pussy was creamy inside, hot, wet and creamy." He licked his lips and I grabbed a hold of him again, even soft he was huge.

After passing out together, we woke up around noon. Neither of us were sure if it was a dream until we realized we were both still naked. "Do you remember Howard, what we did last night?" "Yeah, do you?" "Yeah and holy fuck it was good," I mumbled. "What does this mean," I asked, always the talker. "Whatever you want it to mean Brooke." "I'm not sure Howard. I would never want to lose you and everyone I've been with thus far I've lost." "We can be friends with benefits," he smiled, "we love each other as friends and we have an attraction and neither of us are with anyone else. What's the harm?" "I never expected you to see my body naked, let alone lick it, Howard." "Oh, I have seen it plenty of times when I go to bed at night." "You are a pig Howard." "I know," he laughed.

We tried to go on with the day as normal but something had definitely changed. It wasn't a bad thing but feelings seemed to have changed on both sides.

"Howard, do you think you would've ever done that had we not been drunk and watching half naked women for hours last night?" "Brooke, I've wanted you for a long time. When you were cooking in your bikini, ever since then all I've been thinking about is how it would be with you."

"I've always been curious about you. I must say I'm shocked at how huge you are." "Did you like it," he asked and I said, "I may need a reminder when we're sober," and laughed. The day and night went on and I slept alone in my room. My new job started and I was excited to meet some people and make some money. I worked a combination of days and nights. The nights I had to work, Ed would cook dinner and they would leave me some in the fridge for when I got home.

I had to work a large, prestigious golf banquet today. There were 500 people and they were served the very finest. It was fun but exhausting and my feet were killing me. I had to take my shoes off when the shift was over and drove home barefoot. It was about 9pm when I got home and I just wanted to take a bath and go to bed. Howard was waiting for me to get home; he didn't like to go to sleep until he knew I made it home safe. Good friend.

"How was work Brooke," he asked. "Long and I'm exhausted and my feet are killing me." "I'm going to take a bath." "Okay, do you need any help?" "No, I think I'm good Howard, but thanks for the offer."

Soaking in the hot bath was what my body and feet needed now. I got out of the bath, wrapped a towel around me, and went into my bedroom. Howard was lying on my bed. I asked, "What are you doing?" "I'm waiting for you." "Let me rub your shoulders, I'm sure you're sore." "That would be great, move over." He moved over, I scooted next to him, and he removed the towel I had around me. "Brooke, your skin is so soft." "Thank you, I used whatever was in the shower, it's probably Ed's," we laughed.

He rubbed my shoulders and I turned over on my back and brought him down to kiss me. Within minutes, he was inside me and we were sober and best friends. I grabbed his back with my fingers, leaving scratches from my nails and pulled him further into me. I stared at him and him back at me and rocked back and forth. In that moment, we both knew we were no longer just friends.

"Howard, do you feel different with me now?" "I think so." I agreed. "I think we just made love," I said. "I know we did," he said.

Things were surely different for Howard and me, instead of talking about other lovers we talked about us. It was a gift. We had friendship, trust and great sex. We were having fun while our feelings were growing to new heights.

The phone rang and it was Howard's sister. He was in the bathroom so I answered it. She said, "Who is this," I answered, "Brooke." Is my brother there," she asked? "Yes he's in the bathroom can you hold on a second?" Howard came out of the bathroom and I told him his sister was on the phone and he looked panicked. "Hello," he said. "How long has she been there and why is she there," his sister asked. He told her a few months and she was working down here. His sister told her that his mother wasn't going to be happy.

Noelle and I were friends in high school as well as college and Noelle had a very bad reputation. Howard's family never approved of his friendship with me because they assumed I was like Noelle, which was not the case. Howard never really let it bother him because he knew the truth.

He said nothing when he got off the phone; I just knew that something was wrong. His mother called shortly after and told him that I was no good and that I was a slut just like Noelle and I'll embarrass his family. He would do anything for his mother, he loved her and respected her and she didn't approve. He hung up the phone with his mother and went out for a walk on the beach.

He thought about what his mom and sister said. He knew that they wouldn't make it easy on me, even though he knew those things were not true. He told them that I was nothing like Noelle and we were no longer friends. They had told him they had been getting phone calls about me. He knew they were all lies and nasty things.

Howard got back from his walk and I had already packed, I knew what he was going to say and I didn't want to make it harder on him. "Brooke, I'm sorry, you know how much I care about you," he said. "I get it Howard; I just wish that I didn't get judged on who I used to be friends with. Noelle and I are nothing alike and we never have been. Noelle will stop at nothing to ruin my happiness, as I told you before. I have to believe one day, she will get what's coming to her," I said.

"Howard, I'll miss you, we had so many great times and I have no regrets about what we added, it was great," I said. "Brooke, this shouldn't be happening, this is unfair to you, but you know my family comes first above all," he said. "I'm getting real used to losing anything I love. Howard, I think I'm going to become a Nun." We both laughed and cried at the same time.

"I just wish that I could find someone to love. I want a man that will love me no matter who my friends are and that these losers can't influence. I'm a good person Howard but I'm being punished for that." "Brooke, you're going to make some man very happy and he will be the luckiest guy in the world, don't you ever forget it."

"Good-bye Howard thanks for being a great friend. I just really wish you would have stood up for me a little harder," I said and walked out. "Tell your mom and sisters that I'm one of the good ones, please."

I can't say that I'm angry with Howard. I'm hurt. I understand that they wouldn't want their son with a girl whose reputation is one that they have been lied to about. I'll miss him as a friend more than he'll ever know. I was naive in thinking that this was over with Noelle, Steph and Jonathon. My mind doesn't go to thoughts of hurting people; this is cruelty in a very raw form.

Was all of this because I was with Jonathon and that he actually loved me? Was Noelle in love with Jonathon too? I remember reading in her notebook that he rejected her, is this punishment? Steph lost him when she cheated on him with his friend and then wanted him back. She has him, so why continue to torture me? What is the driving force?

This is going to be a long drive home, 18 hours of internal research. Going back, I loved Jonathon. He was possessive and controlling, but I think he really loved me. It was evident when we were off campus. I did have that one nightstand, I wasn't proud of it, but I needed it. I needed to feel free. Then Ben, he was an amazing man, kind, gentle, honest and they stole that away. Now Howard, my very good friend, they have ended that as well.

I'm now alone, sad, scared and confused. I'm alone without love because of them. This has to stop. This ride is too long with all of these emotions and uncertainty going through my mind. I almost feel like driving over a cliff. Will I ever be allowed to be happy? Will I ever truly have freedom from them? I don't think I can handle this. They have tarnished who I am, and they have hurt people I care about.

I know what I have to do. Only one more hour before I get there. This is going to be the end of this game. I drove up to the park, exhausted and it's now early evening. It's still light out. There it is, the Weeping Willow Tree. I walk to the Willow and sat down underneath and began to strategize. I carved in the tree…. THIS IS OVER! B.W.

This is revenge!

About The Author

Abbey K Davies is married to an amazing man. She has two beautiful children. She lives in a small town in New Hampshire.

She owns a family business and is a Life Coach as well. This is her first book in this genre. She has always dreamt about writing fiction, but never had the courage to do so, until she was faced with a life changing disease that she realized, life is short and one must go after their dreams.

Book 2- REVENGE, part 2 of the Willow Series is available now at Amazon.com

Please check out my other book, The Fire Inside. My new release, FINDNG HOME. I hope you enjoyed this book and read part 2.

abbeykdavies@aol.com

www.abbeykdavies.com

Please feel free to leave a review on Amazon.

PASSION